Brenda Little was born in England and started her writing career by contributing humorous articles to *Punch*. In between selling antiques, running a health-food shop, a marriage, two sons and being a slave to a 200-year-old house she managed to cram in being a newspaper columnist — local history regularly and Pet's Corner and Gardening when there was a crisis in the office. When she broke her foot and had to stay in one place she wrote a novel and it was published. The habit caught on; she wrote three more and they all did quite well. Once in Australia she went back to journalism and wrote for *Vogue*, *Vogue Living* and *Cleo*, was a book reviewer for the *Australian* and had a long stint as a writer for a soapie. There have also been books on art, the consumer society, herbs, organic gardening and three ghost-written stories for survivors of the Holocaust, along with a great deal of editing. *Dear Henry* is her second novel. Brenda is now writing her next novel.

DEAR HENRY

Before her marriage Catherine Fox had been a successful features writer, within an ace of taking over the editorship of Australia's most glossy magazine. Then she met Paul Grant. Four years later, and with three young children, Catherine feels like an unequal partner in their life together. Paul's body seems untouched by fatherhood, but hers is like a stranger's — with lines and marks and bulk where none had been before. Resentments hidden behind politeness do more to poison their relationship than outright anger. Into the domestic drama walks Andromeda the spiky-haired nanny, Janie the glamorous former girlfriend, and Henry . . . dear Henry.

BRENDA LITTLE

DEAR HENRY

Complete and Unabridged

ULVERSCROFT
Leicester

First published in Australia in 2001 by
HarperCollins Publishers Pty Limited
Sydney

First Large Print Edition
published 2002
by arrangement with
HarperCollins Publishers Pty Limited
Australia

British Library CIP Data

Little, Brenda
   Dear Henry.—Large print ed.—
   Ulverscroft large print series: general fiction
   1. Large type books
   I. Title
   823.9'14 [F]

   ISBN 0–7089–4757–3

Published by
F. A. Thorpe (Publishing)
Anstey, Leicestershire

Set by Words & Graphics Ltd.
Anstey, Leicestershire
Printed and bound in Great Britain by
T. J. International Ltd., Padstow, Cornwall

This book is printed on acid-free paper

For Carole, with love

1

She stood in the dark, eyes closed and ears straining, as her mind prowled the rooms above. The house was quiet, murmurous with the breathing of children. Satisfied, she smiled to herself and drifted through to the sitting room.

'They've all gone off,' she said.

'What?'

He was sprawled on the deep couch and surrounded by a spread of newspapers. He did not lift his eyes and continued to read devotedly.

'I said they'd all gone off.'

'Oh.'

She stood and waited, sending out mute claim to his attention. Any minute her steady stare would turn basilisk. She began to count her heartbeats. After four he looked up and caught her narrowed eyes.

'All right, all right, I heard you.'

He was back to his paper almost at once. 'Did you read what bloody Robert Sharp has to say about James's book? Snide isn't the word for it. Listen to this!'

He read for too long with the sonorous

clarity of indignation and then cast the paper from him. 'Critics! They all kid themselves they're God come down from the mountain.'

She would have liked to have read the review but there had been no time today. And there would be no time tomorrow. By Wednesday she would have forgotten all about it and used the paper to wrap up vegetable peelings.

'Jonathon will have something to say about this!' he said, in anticipation.

Jonathon had a great deal to say about everything, that was why she hoped he wouldn't be there tonight.

'You're ready!' she said in alarm, suddenly aware that he was spruce and changed and fragrant with aftershave lotion.

'So how long are you going to be?'

It would take forever to match his careless elegance. 'Ten minutes,' she said.

His flick of a smile avoided her eyes. 'Don't wear those damn trousers, will you? You're not pregnant now, you know.'

She had been intending to wear them; they were cotton, drawstring and comfortable and hid what pregnancies had done to her. Her other clothes belonged to the person motherhood had not overtaken; they hung in the wardrobe, expensive, timeless, elegant, and all too tight under the armpit or

2

uncomfortable under the crotch. She looked wrong in every one of them.

'I don't think I really want to go,' she said.

He groaned and smote his forehead.

'For God's sake! You're always complaining about being housebound and now, when we have an evening out and a sitter organised, you don't really think . . . ' He shook his head at her. 'What are we going to do about you, Cat?'

He had not learnt that you cannot make a palatable brew of reason and irritated condescension. He should have.

'Stuff your evening out — and you too,' she said.

He let the silence drag. It was one of his ploys. She watched him waiting for it to work.

'Then I'd better put the sitter off,' he said at last.

The sitter lived in anxious squalor in a room she could not afford. She was a short-thighed girl with uncooperative hair and a voluble appreciation of life's small mercies. It was her idea of total good fortune to be able to lie on a comfortable couch and watch television with sandwiches and a drink to hand and nothing more required of her than to listen for the awakening of children who seldom stirred once hit by sleep, and to be relied upon to contact the number on the telephone pad should fire break out, burglars erupt into the house or enemies of the State mount a surprise attack.

'The girl can still come. She needs the money.'

'That's stupid!'

'But you will be going.'

'If you don't she won't be needed.'

'Ah, but I have a lovely nature,' she said.

His lips tightened. 'Don't start!'

She didn't, but she wanted to, very badly. The urge to let her words become careless and her voice strident was intense; she could have done full justice to the primeval scream, but there were three young sleepers in the house and she had had enough of them for one day.

'Just go,' she said.

He got up at once.

She let him get as far as the door. She was sure he was secretly pleased to be going without her. 'One thing,' she said. 'I know Janie Gordon will be there. If you were thinking of getting into her knickers again, remember they're a public playground now, so don't forget your old Mum's warnings.'

'God, you can be a bitch when you try!'

'You think I'm *trying*?'

The looks they exchanged were of pure dislike.

4

She listened to the crash of the front door and rasp of his car wheels on the gravel and smiled to herself. 'Enjoy yourself,' she said to him, 'if you can.' With any luck he would be picked up for drinking and driving on the way home. She knew the thought should have shamed her but she did not permit it to do so — if she were a bitch then he had the responsibility for turning her into one, and that was another thing she could hold against him.

They had married four years ago. Attraction had been instant and mutual. But why *marry*? friends had asked, and had been laughed to scorn.

She was twenty-eight and Paul was thirty-two; they had been around and, for both of them, total commitment was beginning to represent sanctuary, not chains, and they each felt it was time to have children. They planned on two but got three; she had become pregnant for the third time when Simon was only six weeks old.

Silently they blamed each other for the monstrous blunder but there had been no talk of abortion; resentments were hidden under careful politeness, which did more to poison their relationship than an outright row. They were equally devoted parents; she had thought they loved each other, but things had gone alarmingly wrong.

The third pregnancy had been unexpectedly difficult. She had vomited throughout the whole nine months and had forgotten what it was like to be without heartburn. She had grown short-tempered and her sunny babies turned into whiners.

'You just don't know how to cope,' Paul had said, impatient with her but patience itself with the children. She resented his competence; she resented his splendid digestion, and even more she resented his unchanged body on which fatherhood had left no mark. Her own body had become grotesque; she carried so much fluid that even her face became puffed. From seven months onwards people in the street regarded her with alarm, as though she were a threat to public decency. She rewarded expectation when her waters broke as she stood at the bank counter.

Barnaby was a large baby and a breech birth; she had been savagely ripped and was cobbled together by a young intern learning his profession. When she left hospital she felt her private parts had become excessively public.

You are making a career out of self-pity, she admonished herself, realising she was going over it all yet again.

She pulled herself together and got out the gin for the sitter, who clearly needed all the indulgences she could get. As further encouragement she spread butter thickly on slices of good wholemeal bread before loading each one with generous helpings of cheese, chopped celery, tomato wedges and chives. She added raisins for good measure, imbedding them with determination so that nourishment should not roll away and be lost to the carpet. She regarded the result with satisfaction; unwieldy to handle, no doubt, but these were very nourishing sandwiches. The sitter, another of whose burdens was the wildly improbable name Andromeda, could not hope to cope with her manifold and manifest misfortunes without the help of vitality. Vitality is a powerful defensive weapon, thought Catherine, too conscious of how much of her own was lost.

Jenny. Simon. Barnaby. Three children in three years. No wonder she felt as though all her strength had been expelled through the birth canal and drained through the paps. She felt no resentment against the children but massive anger against Paul, so unequal a partner in their joint enterprise. He wore his fatherhood with ease and did not conceal his irritation and belief that she made needless heavy weather out of being a mother. He could not — would not, she corrected herself angrily — understand why she had changed so much.

She had always been positive and lively, willing to take life head-on and to laugh at risk; now anxiety was her daily companion. She feared for the children, who were so touchingly vulnerable; she feared death for Paul and herself because the children would be so helpless without them. She now lived surrounded by dangers and threats. Her nerves had become bare wires.

She refused to listen to world news; the suffering, starving children staring out from the television screen reduced her to panic and quiet hysteria. She sent more money than she could afford to the Save the Children Fund and continued to feel helpless and hopeless.

Anxiety was there in the night too. Nothing short of tubal ligation for herself and vasectomy for Paul could have rid her of the fear of being pregnant again. 'Don't be so bloody silly,' he said, annoyed at her insistence on the use of the condom to supplement the protection of the Pill.

She was sharply aware that he turned away, never quite quickly enough, from the sight of the sagging skin across her stomach, and her breasts, flaccid now after so much service. She sometimes suspected he felt anger with himself when physical pressure made him turn to her for relief. As though he were being forced to take necessary but unpalatable medicine, she thought, slamming cupboard doors open and shut.

She glowered at a jar of carob powder, bought for its strength-giving properties but cast aside after one sampling because it took too much strength to stir the damn stuff smooth. It sat there among the packets of kelp, lecithin, brewer's yeast, garlic perles and vitamin capsules, all bought with good intent but left unused because the effort of remembering to take them was too much for her. Her care and concern for the children was unremitting; she didn't seem to have the energy left to look after herself. Better to give the carob powder to the sitter before humidity turned it into a solid lump.

The doorbell rang. Andromeda was never late.

Catherine went to the door, carrying the carob powder jar in her hand. She would slip it into the girl's voluminous and battered hold-all while she remembered it.

Andromeda, looking unlikely, and without anything in which the jar could be slipped,

9

smiled tentatively as she was revealed on the step. 'Surprised?' she asked.

Catherine was stunned. There was far too much eye shadow; trigger-happy scissors had produced the urchin cut, and there was nothing in the world to be done about those short legs, but, for all that . . .

'Coming here,' Andromeda said shyly, 'I mean . . . you are so . . . I thought I ought to try. It would be awful if you were ashamed of me.'

'Come in!' cried Catherine as her spirits took an amused and delighted upward swoop. 'Let me *look* at you!'

She took the girl by the hand and led her through to the sitting room. She saw her own smiling face in the mirror as they passed. She had forgotten her own beauty. I still have my bones, she thought, in an exultant flash. She couldn't wait to pour Andromeda a large gin, but this time she had no thought of making compensation — this girl deserved to be celebrated.

★   ★   ★

It was three in the morning before Paul came in. He smelled of other people. 'The sitter couldn't wait for you to take her home,' she accused him. 'I had to send her by taxi.'

He showed his continued anger with her by

10

silence. When he climbed into bed he kept to his own side as rigidly as though barbed wire lay between them and immediately put out his light. She kept hers on. She knew he found it difficult to sleep unless the room was dark.

Before long his breathing became even and his stiffness sagged into comfort. She was furious to find that neither light nor their discord troubled him sufficiently to keep him awake. It was unfair. He was too impervious by half. She had always risen against injustice, whether it were to tethered dogs, persecuted minorities or timid shoppers who allowed themselves to be queue-jumped. She had been known to be loudly activist in public places. But anger required vitality. She longed for the return of that old red rage, the passionate and missionary zeal. All I can do now is whine, she realised. Even Andromeda, with all the cards stacked against her, has not fallen apart as I have. Let's hope the vitamin pills I insisted we took after munching our way through that pile of health-giving sandwiches have a salutary effect. It's time something did.

She found she was thinking of Andromeda with amused affection; it was the first soothing thought to come her way for some time. She enjoyed it. As she slid into sleep she also enjoyed the knowledge that Paul would be furious when he found that she had charged the cost of Andromeda's taxi to his account.

2

'Do you mind?' Catherine asked.

Shoppers should shop, not coagulate into a gossiping group that denied progress to others with little time to shop and none at all to gossip.

'Do you *mind*?' she said again, her voice lost in the soothing Muzak which was proving such a failure in intent.

The baby was papoosed to her back, and Simon and Jenny, crammed into the stroller, were engaged in a silent and slit-eyed foot fight which threatened to dislodge the gaping packages jammed around them.

I must look like a one-woman refugee camp, she thought savagely. Any minute now someone would give her that look of smug and superior pity she had come to dread. No wonder true refugees stared into television cameras in so inimical a fashion.

'Do you *mind*?' she said yet again. Her voice had taken a dangerous lift. She gave the stroller a forward shove. The jarring contact with flesh was intensely satisfying.

The woman blocking her path turned angrily. 'Look where you're going, you stupid bitch!'

'Just get out of my way, will you?'

It was a demand, not a request. The woman shifted at once and glared in resentment.

There was no time to apologise and explain that she was so desperate for a pee that good manners were out of the question. She was obsessed by the necessity to get back to the car park, where she would have to manhandle two heavy children into their car seats and buckle them in, heft the baby into his capsule, collapse the stroller and transfer it and all the shopping into the boot, before scrambling into the car and driving like hell for home, where, with any luck, she might be able to crouch behind the bushes in the drive before her tortured bladder gave out on her.

This was another of the perks of motherhood. Barnaby had been butchered out of her and God alone knew what damage had been done. Now she leaked whenever she laughed and standing and walking had become hazardous. She lived in fear that she might stink in spite of all the care she took. She was certain that, one time, pressure would make her wet all over Paul and their marital bed and that his present distaste for her would turn into a final disgust. She was forever trying to balance intake against output, time against capacity. She had miscalculated badly this time.

The car was on the far side of the park, under the trees. She had purposely left it there try to and keep the interior as cool as possible, for she knew well what the all-too-close encounter in the stroller did to the children's tempers and what leather seats, unprotected against the sun, could do to half-naked small bodies. The damn thing seemed miles away.

She hurried.

The jarring of her heels against the concrete invited disaster. She broke out into a sweat, knowing that time was against her. The splashy whisper of the fountain, installed no doubt to give a little dignity to the lurid commercialism of the shopping complex, sent her into a panicky detour to avoid it. Bloody planners; she ought to write to them to complain. She was half laughing, half whimpering when, at last, she fumbled the key into the car-door lock.

She unslung the baby from her back. As she brought him forward he hung limp in her arms, his head rolled back. Under the fan of his eyelashes the skin looked blue.

How soon could babies dehydrate?

'Barnaby!' she cried, shaking him. In panic she slapped at his pale cheek.

His eyes flew wide. He took a deep,

shuddering breath as his bottom lip turned down and his mouth squared up. He was neither dead nor dehydrated, but outraged and about to show it.

She was shaking violently as she bundled him into his capsule and closed the door on his cries. 'Shut up!' she shouted to him, through the glass.

The stupid way you overreact, Paul often said. Well, he wasn't here to say it now.

The children shrank away from her and were lumpy and uncooperative as she hauled them from the stroller.

'Get in,' she said grimly, shoving them into seats and safety belts.

She had still to deal with the stroller and the shopping.

Pain struck just as she had everything in the boot. It tingled, white-hot, through the whole of her body and took her breath away. She felt goose bumps come up on the back of her arms. She closed her eyes and bent over double, clutching at herself.

It seemed forever before the agony began to pass and she could straighten up. As she opened her eyes she became aware of the hot trickle down the inside of her legs. How would she ever dare to move? Facing her in the boot was a packet of disposable nappies she had bought for Barnaby. She snatched at it, slammed the boot shut and hobbled round to the driver's seat. In the haven of the car she ripped the packet open and crammed a nappy between her legs and between her and the car seat. Her teeth were chattering as the bursting flow gave exquisite relief. She used all her strength on her bladder muscles to hurry release from the unbearable pressure. She heard her own long, keening moan as she came back to herself and faced the problem of her sodden clothing and three wailing children. She leaned her head against the steering wheel and added her sobs to theirs. She felt utterly humiliated.

Oblivious to everything she cried herself out. When she at last gave a final exhausted gasp and lifted her head she looked right into the face of a man bending to peer at her through the open window.

'Piss off!' she hissed, in outrage.

He tutted and shook his head in gentle reproof. 'Now, now. No need to be rude. I just wondered if anything was wrong.'

Couldn't he see the state of her? Couldn't he hear the children?

'Of course there bloody well is!' she rasped, and reached for the car keys.

There were no keys; they were in the lock of the boot. Her hand fell to her lap and encountered the sodden bulk. She turned her face away. 'Just *go!*' she said through her teeth.

He did not move. She could feel him looming.

'I'll pass you your keys first,' he said.

He must have been watching her. How much had he seen? She waited in clenched misery.

When he handed her the keys his placid, middle-aged face gave nothing away; his smile was easy.

'Thanks,' she managed to say.

'Drive carefully.'

There was such powerful kindness in his words that she crumpled at once, but she was damned if she would cry again.

'I was rude, I'm sorry.'

'S-ssh.'

He was obviously a practised soother. She wished she could use his blend of tenderness and authority on her own children.

'But I am. Really.'

'Think nothing of it,' he said, giving the car door a valedictory pat. 'Nobody's perfect.'

She sat and watched him walk away. He was a big, ungainly man. He turned his feet out when he walked and showed too much sock. She had a sudden mental picture of what he must look like in just his underpants and her heart warmed to him. She made a special point of hooting and waving as she drove away. The brief smiles they had exchanged seemed more intimate than any she had shared for a long time. She laughed to herself as she swung the car out into the traffic. Life no longer seemed tragic, just ludicrous.

The children settled down as she sped along the freeway and her nerves eased. By the time she had made the sweep up to the plateau and home, all her annoyance was concentrated on manufacturers who claimed an absorption rate for their product it clearly did not have.

As she pulled up in the drive she saw a large florist's basket standing in the shade by the front door.

Paul? A peace offering?

The card attached read, 'For everything, Andromeda.' The flowers must have cost the girl all she had earned last night, and more.

She was *damned* if she would cry *again*. But she did.

When she had calmed down she was confusedly aware that she seemed to have shed more than tears, but, with three children to cope with, there was no time to examine this new lightness of heart.

Barnaby slept, the other two children played and she enjoyed her own rendering of

19

the humming chorus from 'Butterfly' as she hard-boiled eggs, cut up zucchini and broccoli and made cheese sauce. She had forgotten to go to the butcher's and she was delighted. She could now thwart Paul's appetite for red meat. He deserved to be punished. She did not forgive him for the indignities of the morning. Not only had he brought her to this, but he had left her alone with it.

He was the last person she could tell about what had happened; he would not help her, with either humour or love, to accept such embarrassing fallibility.

His fastidiousness would make him shrink away from the vulgar weakness of organs he did not wish to know she had. But I am *forced* to know, she thought. Nature allows men delicacy but affords us women none.

She was glad the dish looked so pallid and uninteresting. Better a dish of herbs, she would tell him, and offer it with a slanted smile. *And* she would be wearing her comfortable, cotton, drawstring pants.

It seemed that she had not lost her laughter after all; it was just that the nature of it was changed.

3

She had guessed there must be something dodgy about it; the advertisement had been in the paper far too long.

GARDEN FLAT. SUIT BUSINESS GIRL. LOW RENT and a Peninsula number to contact should have ensured an immediate snapping up but obviously nobody had snapped.

Andromeda had been to the Peninsula once, on a school-leavers' outing two years ago, and had been in rebellion against Blacktown ever since. Palm Beach! Whale Beach! Avalon! Bilgola! had become her litany. To think that people actually *lived* on that magic finger of land with the ocean on one side of its elegant length and the blue peace of Pittwater on the other. There was so much light, so many cliffs and frilled bays, so many bobbing boats and so much lush greenery; tousled-haired, half-naked shoppers spilled out of expensive cars, houses hung between sea and sky — it was heaven. Her favourite reading became real-estate descriptions of property for sale there.

'For Christ's sake,' her sister had said. 'It's

the jobs vacant columns you should be looking at. You've been unemployed six months now. You wouldn't catch me without work. You just don't try.'

But Andromeda had tried and she was sour with finding that someone else was always chosen to mind the machines, clean the offices or serve customers.

'And I'll be wanting your bedroom. You can't expect Jonquil and Darren to go on sharing. It isn't decent.'

She knew it wasn't. She had heard the nocturnal rustling and sniggering. Her sister had her own dreams and a scandal on her hands would wreck all her pretensions. They would be wrecked sooner or later, shared bedroom or not, but at least she would not be around to face accusations.

'I'll go,' she had said, and answered the dodgy advertisement.

★ ★ ★

The 'garden flat' turned out to be the back room of a dilapidated weekender in overgrown bush, well back from the coast. No business girl in her right mind would have considered it. The loo and primitive cold-water shower were up in the garden.

'We all used to come here in the old days,'

the woman said defensively. 'Us kids had great fun here.'

She clearly wasn't having any now. Her husband had left her, their home had been sold and fifty-odd was not the best time to start making a new life.

'Thank God I had this place,' she sighed.

Andromeda thought it was little enough to thank Him for and enjoyed an unaccustomed sense of superiority. She might not have been chosen by a member of the opposite sex but she had never been publicly rejected.

'It might do,' she said in her best voice, 'though it is a long way from the road.'

'Electricity's included . . . '

'I thought it was *your* telephone number — I expected there to be a phone.'

The discussion was superfluous. They both knew she was going to take it and they both hoped like hell that she would be able to keep up with the rent on her unemployment benefit. Don't try and spoof me, love, the tired eyes had warned and Andromeda had given up the attempt at once.

'Thank God you're not a smart-arse. I've seen enough of *them*.'

She was so prone to give thanks that Andromeda found it catching. Although the tattered flyscreens would give no protection at all against mosquitoes intent on ravaging her city flesh, she could rejoice in the scent of frangipani which drenched the room. Divan (comfortable), armchair (elderly), table (rickety), dining-chair (hard) and small electric cooking stove (filthy) were all that was offered, but the view was magnificent.

'Don't get carried away,' the woman said drily. 'We face right into the southerlies.'

'How much is the bond?'

'How much do you reckon?'

'I don't know. I've never done this before.'

'No more have I. When d'you want to move in?'

'But I don't know if . . . '

'Oh, shut up and go and get your bits and pieces,' Dulcie Tims had said.

'At least you won't be a pest with lads after you all hours of the night.'

Dulcie was a lump of a woman, kind, tactless beyond bearing and charmless beyond belief. She wore splayed white sandshoes and a flowered pinafore of a type off the market years ago. The wonder was that any man would have married her, let alone left her. She made a marvellous landlady, though. Basins of fish soup and Glad-wrapped slices of cold meat would appear on the rickety table now covered by an Indian cloth. Copies of the local newspaper with possible jobs ringed were left on the step.

24

'Don't take nothing *they* could find out about!' was the advice given.

On pension-cheque days she went down to the village to do her fortnightly shopping. It was Andromeda's dread that they might meet in the street. Dulcie left off her apron on shopping days but nothing would part her from her sandshoes. She wore a child's flowered sunhat and backpacked her shopping in an army surplus rucksack. Public association with such an obvious ratbag was beyond Andromeda. Conscious of being so near to one herself, she avoided Dulcie in private as well as in public, as though her condition might be catching.

The ringed jobs in the paper always went to somebody else but at least she was not sour about it now. She had chosen the right place in which to be poor. The sun and the sea were free. Every day she tramped down to the village, bought fruit and went to sit on the little beach below the cliffs. Every day she toasted herself devotedly and smugly shared long, golden afternoons with young mothers, as satin with oil as they were, though not as smooth with privilege. She watched everything. She particularly noticed a pregnant woman who wore a sarong around her thickened body as stylishly as she wore her long hair wrapped around her perfectly shaped skull. When she called to her children her voice was everything Dulcie Tims was not. When she no longer came, Andromeda missed her. Not that she thought they would ever have the slightest thing in common.

The day they actually met Andromeda had been limping away from the beach and feeling fraught. All the walking had worn her sandals through and she could not afford another pair; she would have to go into thongs. She hated them as much as she loved nice shoes; she had pretty feet. But thongs it would have to be, for she had to pay her rent. Dulcie's finances were balanced on as much of a knife-edge as her own.

When she looked up Catherine had been coming down the path; she was panting and leaning heavily on the stroller. She was dreadfully changed. Andromeda had averted her eyes politely. Anyone looking like *that* would prefer to be unseen. Catherine had obviously felt no such need. As they came close Andromeda had been astonished to hear her sudden bark of laughter.

'The halt and the lame!' Catherine had said, puffing out her already puffed-out cheeks. 'What a pair we make! I hardly have to tell you what happened to me. What happened to you?'

Andromeda had seen the gallant good

humour in the ravaged face, been amazed and charmed by the easy familiarity, and the obsession began.

★   ★   ★

Now, many months later, she lay in the sun outside her room and thought back. She had scrubbed and cleaned everything scrubbable and cleanable; virtue was hers; she could relax.

'You've took up my carpet,' said Dulcie Tims, a sudden shadow, blocking the sun. 'And what have you done with my table?'

'I'm going Japanese,' Andromeda said and waited for Dulcie to say God Almighty. They had developed a stable relationship.

'God Almighty,' Dulcie said obligingly. 'You're turning into a right crackpot. And what time did you get in last night?'

'Late. I came by taxi.'

'God Almighty,' Dulcie said again. 'I hope you didn't pay for it.'

'Of course not.'

'Why didn't he bring you like always?'

'He was still out.'

'Oho.'

Dulcie lived off such morsels of information. She could smell trouble quicker than a Customs dog could smell out dope, and was happy in her work.

'That's what I thought,' ventured Andromeda, feeling treachery towards Catherine but still prepared to use her as strategy. 'All right if I cut the legs of the table down?'

'Eh?'

'I told you. I'm going Japanese.'

'Crackpot. Did she come home by herself then?'

'She didn't go.'

'Eh?'

Dulcie's fascination was total. Now was the time to ask if she minded if the divan legs were sawn down too.

'She suggested it. She lent me this saw. And she gave me some clothes too.'

'Eh?'

She had made Dulcie's day. All things were possible now.

'Well, come on then.' Dulcie said. 'Aren't you going to show me? And keep your flaming saw off my chairs though. You can sit on your bum, same as the Nips do.'

Andromeda showed her. There were two dresses, a shirt and a skirt. 'Will you help me do the shortening?'

'God Almighty,' said Dulcie, with real reverence. 'She gave you *these*? Then you're not the only one off your onion.'

* * *

Sawing was not as easy as she had thought and it took a long time to make sure each leg was the same length. It became a very low, low table.

Andromeda sang as she worked and picked up thoughts interrupted by Dulcie. She often went over it all and always with the same pleasure.

When she met Catherine for the first time she had helped push the children home.

'I had to bring them down to the beach,' Catherine had said. 'They pestered so. God knows how I'm going to get them back home.'

The house had overwhelmed Andromeda.

'But you've got a *pool*!' she cried.

There was even a diving board.

'It's six metres deep. And kids like sand.'

The huge balcony looked out over the valley, the cliffs and the sea.

'Can you imagine the drop?' Catherine had said.

The ceiling of the main room went up to the rafters. Stairs led to a second-floor gallery where doors opened into other rooms. The bottom of the stairway was blocked off by a pile of cardboard boxes.

'They'd fall over there too,' Catherine had said. 'I have to try to keep them in the playroom and the kitchen.'

She did not appear to be very successful. Simon and Jenny were active and determined children. Coping with them and her bulk was clearly beyond Catherine.

'*Siddown!*' Andromeda had found herself saying. The children had subsided into silence and immobility.

Catherine had looked at her with round eyes. 'How would you like to be our sitter?' she asked, and had opened heaven.

She was expected to find her own way to the house but Mr Grant ran her home. She asked to be dropped at the end of the lane. She did not think Mr Grant would find Dulcie compatible. Mr Grant. She could not be familiar with him even in her thoughts. He seldom spoke to her on the drive home. 'Why did they call you Andromeda?' he once asked and all she could say was 'I don't know' and that was the end of that.

'When you say 'Mrs Grant' I look round for my mother-in-law,' Catherine had insisted. 'My name is Catherine and my husband is Paul.'

But not to me, Andromeda had thought. And Mr Grant would not want to be 'Paul' to me.

Although she had seen his underwear on the washing line and had once heard him fart as she passed the downstairs loo, he remained above and beyond her.

It was not that his name often appeared in the newspapers and that she had often seen him being interviewed on television — she could have easily fallen into first-name terms with many a person who appeared on the box, for it was only luck that had separated them from the mob — but Mr Grant was different. He knew his place and he knew his rights — and they did not include being called 'Paul' by the babysitter.

I'm not daft, Andromeda told herself, though it often seemed that Catherine was.

'Anyone would think you were born a Pom, not me,' she had heard her shout. 'What's wrong with her calling me 'Catherine'?'

'If you don't know there's no point in telling you,' the quiet voice had responded and a door had slammed. Doors slammed quite often lately. Every time they did, benefits seemed to fall on Andromeda.

They'll be slamming again after last night, she mused, though what further blessings could come her way she could not imagine.

4

Janie Gordon stood by her office window and looked out over the city she loved. The warm, coloured blur of the suburbs ran out beyond sight; down below in the canyoned grid of streets the familiar flow of traffic pulsed and oozed. She knew every sign on every tall building; she knew which lanes on the Harbour Bridge would be closed at this time of day; she knew which windows would suddenly flash fire as the sun sank a little lower. By the harbour waters the white and lovely lunacy of the Opera House made the picture which said 'home'. She hated to think she had been here too long but all the signs gave warning it was time to go. When somewhere becomes full of 'places' and a restaurant has ceased to be just a restaurant but has become a haunt, something has to be done. She had been a fool too long.

'If anyone rings, say I'm not in,' she said.

'What makes you think he'll ring?' asked her secretary, to whom all things were known.

Janie turned from the window. 'I saw him at James's last night.'

'You idiot! You knew he'd be there. Why did you go?'

'Just say I'm not here. Tell him anything. Say I've gone down with the clap. It's what he's expecting to hear anyway.'

Eve Castle made a high, keening noise. She had been with Janie a long time and their relationship was a compound of love and exasperation.

'If you cry over that bastard you can get yourself another secretary.'

'Promises, promises.'

They smiled at each other affectionately and then Janie's smile died.

What am I going to *do*? she asked herself.

She should have been over Paul Grant by now. Might have been. But he was always around.

There are only seven people in Australia and they all know each other, the English-born Catherine Fox had joked. She had come out with a lot of other smart-alec things too and looked under her lashes as she said them. She was lovely and she had flair. How I liked her, Janie thought with familiar sickness, remembering how instinctive friendship had been. She was so much more alive than most people; I *enjoyed* her. I liked the way she threw down challenges and grinned when they were picked up.

She had challenged Paul Grant, who no longer found challenge in his long-time love, Janie Gordon.

Catherine knew what she wanted and, though her glance at Janie had been rueful and apologetic, she had been forthright and staked her claim. Paul had been happy to be claimed.

'She's as tired of the merry-go-round as I am,' he had said in bland explanation. 'After all there does come a time to settle down.'

'You didn't ask me if I wanted to settle down.'

'You!' His surprise had been genuine. For a second she wondered if she saw regret.

He had always come and gone — his toothbrush a regular visitor too, rather than a permanent fixture in her bathroom. She had left clothes of hers to hang with his in his wardrobe. They were invited everywhere as a couple — the relationship had the feeling of stability. The rope holding them was not tight but it seemed strong.

It is a mistake to play the role one thinks is required, she reflected. I played successful businesswoman to his successful business-man; my demands on him were light so that should he stray, as I knew he would, he would be happy to come back. He always did. I thought I was being clever. But he did not

34

come back from his encounter with Catherine Fox.

Everyone commented on how well I handled it. 'Janie is so good-natured,' they said. No harsh words to Paul, and to Catherine best wishes and the light quip, 'I only did four years but you have a life sentence!' No betrayal of the knowledge that both friend and lover were lost, for closeness with either was now impossible.

She remembered Catherine's face when they first met. Lovely though it was, lines were showing around her eyes. She had noticed them at once. She is no longer young, she had thought, and knew that Catherine was aware of it too. The suspicion that she might have married Paul for the wrong reasons made acceptance difficult.

At least the lines round her own eyes were no deeper than they had been, although the time since Paul had been turbulent. He seemed to be aware of where the wild water had taken her.

'I've been hearing things about you,' he had remarked. 'You disappoint me.'

Too many of his friends had known her bed and he was afraid comparison might have been made and laughter shared. Paul set value on performance. He was a skilled engineer and took pride in his expertise.

I could only feed his self-love, she concluded, but Catherine Fox could make him vulnerable.

When she was in hospital having their first child he had been distraught.

'What if anything happens to her?' he had said.

He had been in her bed when he said it but they both knew that hardly signified — he was not used to sleeping alone and habit had brought him there. She hated herself for living with the hope that it might again. She had recognised the signs of strain in him. Paul is not happy, she had thought, and felt pleasure.

She did not like herself for it.

And one thing was for sure, he need not look to her for comfort.

And yet, I cannot let go, she agonised. What is it I want from him? Do I need him to need *me* again so that I can get back my self-respect? Do I need to draw blood to punish him for the way he was able to leave me behind with the casualness with which one discards yesterday's newspaper?

Curiously she felt less animosity towards Catherine Fox, the thief, than towards the man who had allowed himself to be stolen.

The telephone rang.

'The Gordon Agency,' Eve said. 'Who is calling, please?'

Her eyebrows shot up as she listened. 'I'm sorry,' she said, vowels round, 'Miss Gordon has left the office. Can I take a message for her?'

It seemed that she could not and her mouth went down at the corners as she replaced the phone. She glared at Janie.

'Don't give me all that wild surmise!' she said. 'What the hell have you been up to? That wasn't *him*. That was *her*.'

★ ★ ★

Shame and curiosity had driven Catherine to the telephone. She regretted the cheap crack about Janie Gordon she had made to Paul. She had always admired her. Paul had been enhanced in value because he found favour with such a splendid girl. Taking him away from her had been feathers in the bonnet but today's Catherine could find no pleasure in the achievement. She put the receiver down and felt bleak.

It was a mistake to give my name, she thought. She never will be in to me.

I know I still fight against her, using innuendo and mockery, and I know she thinks of me with black dislike, but of all the people in the world we are the two who should band together. She should know it too.

She picked up the phone with new determination.

'This is Catherine Grant again,' she said crisply. 'Please ask Miss Gordon to ring me as soon as she gets to the office in the morning. She will know my number. No, you *cannot* tell her what it is about.'

She put the receiver down on the squawk from the other end of the wire. Bloody secretaries, mommas every one, living life at second hand, but oh, how missed when they were no longer there. It takes two women to cope with one woman's life, she mused. Janie still has her support but where is mine? Dolly came with the job and went with it, taking her black-hearted humour to some other woman battling it out in the public arena. But the real battles are fought on the private front, where the terms are even more unequal.

The impulse to ring Janie had been mindless. Now, if she rang back, what was there to say?

'Come to lunch'? Impossible. Paul would be furious.

'Let's have lunch together'? Equally impossible. How do you conduct a meaningful encounter while coping with three small children?

A meaningful encounter, she mocked herself. How stupid can you get? I have to do better than this.

But she could not. When she tried to think clearly it was as though the two halves of her mind would no longer mesh together. Lost in confusion and the jangling of her nerves, all she could do was to send out a soundless cry for help, which shamed her. How had she, once so positive and sunny, become such a mess?

She proved what a mess she was by again turning first-class ingredients into a third-class meal, which she and Paul ate in their separate, angry silences.

'I'm going to bed,' he announced soon afterwards and left her to watch the imbecilities of television. She stared stolidly until after midnight, punishing herself. This was all she rated.

★   ★   ★

All through the dark hours possums raged and fought in the big mango tree outside the children's bedroom window. The hissing and demonic scolding brought Catherine up from uneasy sleep and she lay and fumed, praying

39

the children would not wake.

Prayer had no power against such primitive screams of rage. Simon's cot bars began to rattle; any minute now he would wake Jenny.

'Come on,' she said to Paul, urgently.

She was out of bed, with the light on, but he still slept.

'Paul!'

Both children were wailing now, bewildered, beseeching cries that wrenched her gut. Bloody animals. With miles of bush around why should they choose to vandalise her garden and terrify her children?

He was at her side within a breath of waking. This was one area in which she could not fault him. 'You take Simon, I'll take Jenny,' he said.

Pacing, patting, crooning, they passed each other, up and down the bedroom as the mad rustle in the breaking branches and unearthly savagery went on. Under his mosquito net Barnaby slept like a small stone image.

'There, there,' Paul soothed, 'don't be frightened. Daddy's got you.'

Jenny was octopused to his chest, strangling her way to safety. Simon, wet with sweat, kept up a high-pitched scream as he dug his feet into Catherine's stomach and butted his head against her shoulder.

'For God's sake, give him to me,' Paul said.

They exchanged children with difficulty.

I just hope we are frightening the possums, Catherine thought, giving thanks there were no near neighbours.

It took time before the children were soothed sufficiently to be tucked back in their beds.

Paul leant over and stroked Jenny's hair. 'There we are, sweetheart. Nothing to be frightened about. It was only the nice little possums.'

'Stop stuffing her up with lies,' Catherine hissed. 'They're horrible little beasts.'

His hand was ungentle at her shoulder as he propelled her back to their own room.

'Do you want to set them off again?'

'They wouldn't have started in the first place if you'd sent for the ranger when I asked you. They've been around for a week now.'

He could remember the name of people met only once, he had the telephone numbers of all his contacts by heart, but let her ask him to do a simple thing like bring home a carton of milk or make a call for her and his splendid memory failed him entirely.

'I suppose I will have to get him myself,' she added, laying blame.

'You won't need him. That was probably a

strange young male, ours will have scared him off.'

'Ours?'

It was an old area of dispute.

We can give them space, he had said, when the possums first made their presence known — after all they were here before we were. She had liked his charitableness and had put out food for them. Now they pissed in the roof, ate her geranium flowers and took bites out of half-ripe mangoes. One day one fell down the chimney and, blacked with soot and mad with fright, had fouled carpets, ripped curtains, overturned flower vases and scratched her so badly she needed stitches and a tetanus shot. Just bad luck, Paul had insisted. He had not shared her conviction that she faced death by blood-poisoning.

'Don't start that paranoid nonsense again,' he said now. 'We've lost enough sleep.'

'And half our mangoes. Doesn't it upset you to see the children so frightened? Doesn't the damage they do bother you?' She could not keep the sob out of her voice.

'Cat, Cat,' he said with tired indulgence, and took her in his arms.

He stroked well. He found all the tense places. They stood and rocked together in the dawn-streaked light, their bodies settling together with the old effortless ease.

Her anger against him drained away in a long sigh. All she needed to make her whole was his kindness, a temporary loan of his strength. Her lips opened against his neck in a blind burrowing for sustenance.

'Silly old Cat,' he murmured. 'Why have you become so impossible?'

He led her to their bed. She settled into his arms with tired gratitude. Now they could sleep with all differences forgotten and tomorrow they might even be the people they used to be. 'Darling,' she said, already drifting.

She felt his erection stir against her thigh. He reached for her hand and drew it downwards.

'We may as well use the time. I won't be able to go back to sleep again.'

She let him use his time on her; after all they owed their standard of living to his aversion to the wasted moment.

When he rolled off her, without climax, she felt vindictive pleasure.

'What the hell's the matter with you?'

She said nothing.

He flung himself out of bed and wrenched open the balcony door. She saw his hunched shoulders, black against the stained sky as he leaned on the rail and stared out over the valley. He was too edgy to be still for long.

'I asked what's the matter with you,' he repeated, coming back to the bed.

She lay, spread and uncovered, silk bunched about her waist. She accused him by her limp, open thighs and naked lovelessness.

The sun eased up from the sea, filling the room with light. She watched his anger grow and measured her silence against it. Their locked stares held. At last he made a brusque, exasperated gesture and turned away in distaste. 'For God's sake, woman,' he said, 'cover yourself up,' and left her.

After a time, with cold precision, she drew her limbs together and drew the sheet over them. I should have known better, she told herself.

She took long, deep, careful breaths. She drew life into herself, held it, and monitored the ebb with exquisite control. Gradually the two halves of her mind, which for so long had seemed unable to mesh, began to move together. They locked. The frisson of pleasure was deeper and more satisfying than any pleasure the body could offer. She lay quiet and let the new strength and malevolence take hold.

★ ★ ★

'Mrs Tims knows a possum man,' Andromeda informed her the next morning.

'Then for God's sake ask her to tell him to
come round here as soon as possible.'

To hell with Paul. She could deal with her
own problems.

5

'You're surely not going to ring her?'

Janie put the phone down. 'If I don't she will certainly ring me.'

'Then tell her to get stuffed.'

'You don't tell Catherine Fox things like that.'

'The name is Catherine *Grant*,' Eve Castle said acidly. 'Don't tell me you've forgotten.'

'Leave it, will you?' Janie asked, without hope. Eve could be as obsessive in pursuit of a point as she was in search of lost documents and forgotten names. She was at her most determined now.

'The way you clutch at straws is indecent. You'd do anything to keep in touch with that bloody Paul! For an intelligent woman you behave like the biggest fool of all time. Dammit, Janie, he's the father of three children.'

'I know.'

'Then why do you still think of him as the fella you were with for four years? He doesn't exist any more.'

But he does, Janie thought. I saw him the other night and he saw me.

'*Leave* it,' she said, finding authority.

There was work to be done. The pictured faces of the beautiful people who depended on her for a living stared at her from the walls. The responsibility was always with her. She could hide behind it now. She avoided Eve's eyes and picked up a file.

'Can't we try for a voice-over for Bonnie Passmore? She won't be fit to dance again for six months, and the truck driver who knocked her down wasn't insured.'

'Thank God for Bonnie Passmore. At least she doesn't suffer from self-inflicted wounds.'

Eve had a right to impatience; she was having to watch her sister die from cancer and it gave her a stern sense of priorities.

'I won't ring her,' Janie said impulsively, remembering.

Eve grunted and got on with her work. Her lips stayed thin.

I wish I could say I find my troubles piddling because yours are so great, Janie thought, but one pain never cancels out another, it just adds to the malaise. I am as willing to be rid of what eats me as your sister must be to be rid of what eats her, and we are both helpless. Despise me, as you must, but don't ask me to give up the one gleam of hope to come my way in a long time. And don't ask what I hope for. I don't know. But I do know something is afoot and I want to know what it is because it might rid me of the debilitating sense of living with unfinished business.

'Could Bonnie make mineral water sound sexy?' Eve asked.

'She managed it with laxatives.'

The telephone rang. It was not Catherine Grant.

The day settled into the familiar pattern of anxieties, demands, and fervent thanks. Janie functioned at her admirable best, consciously striving for Eve's approval.

She won it. Eve dropped a kiss in the air above Janie's head as she was leaving. 'You only let me bully you because you know I'm right,' she said.

★   ★   ★

When she had gone Janie dialled Catherine's number. It was four-thirty, a time mothers of young children would surely consider tea-time.

Catherine obviously did not.

Where the hell has she been all day? Janie wondered.

She had telephoned at a quarter to nine that morning, a strategic fifteen minutes before Eve was due to arrive. There had been no answer then either. At that hour, with three children, she must have been *up* but was highly unlikely to be out, so what the hell was she playing at? How dare she be so bloody rude?

Easily, the answer came. She would have learnt from Paul that, with Janie, one could get away with anything.

But not this time!

You may get away with things between you and me, she told the ever-present face in her mind, but there is no way in the world you can be allowed to teach another human being to undervalue me. Particularly not Catherine Fox.

It was the first time she had felt hostile towards him. It came on her with a physical spasm as definite as the one which, each month, declared her ovulation. It was the most primitive emotion she had felt in their complicated relationship.

How about that? she thought in slow, pleased amusement.

'I can see why you might be in love with him,' Eve had once declared, 'but sure as hell I'll never know what you find to *like* in him.'

Eve was sharp. She knew how to needle. Janie kept thinking about the remark all the way home.

During the evening she sat and listened to

André Previn playing Gershwin and, with her best dressmaking scissors, cut the pyjama jacket Paul had left behind into very neat, very small pieces.

★　★　★

Catherine had forgotten all about Janie.

The exhausted children had slept late so she had ample time to provide Paul with the sort of breakfast he liked but seldom got. He left without eating it.

She consigned the perfectly cooked bacon, eggs delicately shrouded in their whites, and the nutty toast to the waste bin, and smiled. She roused the children, fed them, packed all three into the car and was on her way to Andromeda by half past eight.

'It's hard to find,' Andromeda had once said, giving her address with reluctance.

It was proving damn near impossible to find. Surely no one would have built a house up here amongst this tangle of lantana and scrubby she-oaks snarled over with rampant morning glory. As the car lurched and jolted up the runnelled, rutted road Catherine began to understand why Paul looked so martyred when required to take Andromeda home. This road was bad enough in daylight; it must be hell at night. Now broken branches

50

of angophora were littering the path, which was clearly giving out. He did not bring her all this way, that was for sure. He would never subject his beloved Mercedes to the punishment. Now there was only sky ahead.

'Bloody ridiculous,' she muttered, wrenching the wheel to avoid a jutting rock. But at least she seemed to have arrived. A dilapidated weatherboard house came into view and a bulky woman, fearsome in dressing-gown, sandshoes and flowered hat, was barring the way.

'No road!' cried Dulcie Tims, peremptory as a policewoman, lifting her arms and presenting Catherine with the flat of her forbidding hands.

'I can see that,' said Catherine crossly as Dulcie came around to the driver's window.

This could only be the landlady about whom Andromeda was so reticent. It was difficult to know where to look.

'I want to see Andromeda Brown.'

'God Almighty — at this time in the morning!'

'Yes,' said Catherine, establishing her authority.

She and Dulcie eyed each other.

'Aha,' exclaimed Dulcie, pointing a finger, 'Mrs Grant!'

'Yes.'

Dulcie slapped the roof of the car. 'Get your brake on then. Follow me.'

As Catherine scrambled from the car Barnaby began to wail.

'It'll soon shut up,' Dulcie said, plodding round the side of the house.

Andromeda was discovered in her nightdress in the lotus position facing the morning sun. She had difficulty unscrambling her limbs.

'Mrs Grant!'

'I want to talk to you.'

'Then I'd better be off,' said Dulcie affably. 'God knows how you got the car up here and God knows how you'll get it back again. We're not on the phone — in case you were thinking of sending for the NRMA.'

'I'm sorry,' said Andromeda as Dulcie lumbered round to her own side of the house. 'I never *thought* . . . I mean . . . '

'Never mind all that. I have the children in the car. I can't waste time.'

Andromeda waved a flustered hand indicating the doorway of her room. 'Do you want to come *in*?'

She clearly thought it territory unfit for Catherine's eyes.

'No . . . '

'Then can I make you a cup of coffee? It's only instant . . . '

'Do shut up,' said Catherine. 'Just listen. How would you like to come and live with us?'

Andromeda gave a small, mewling cry and spread her hands.

'Not *with* us, exactly. There's a room over the garage. You could use the poolroom shower. You would be quite separate. I need you,' she added, on a higher, exasperated note, 'to help me to look after the children.'

This girl was annoyingly slow on the uptake.

'I thought you needed a job,' she pressed.

'I do. I do. But what about her?'

'Who?'

'Mrs Tims.'

'That woman? What about her?'

'She needs my rent,' Andromeda said in a small, suffering voice.

'For heaven's sake! She could get another tenant.'

'No, she couldn't.'

Catherine looked around. Ineffectually concealed by a low bush a dunny leaned, the door swinging open; behind Andromeda the details of the 'Japanese' room were clearly revealed.

'All right then. Keep the damn place on. You can come back at weekends. How much is the rent?'

Andromeda told her.

How could anyone *need* so small an amount of money?

'Well that's no problem; you'll have more than enough for that. You won't need anything for food and you can still collect your unemployment benefit.'

'But I'd be working for you!'

'So what? Who's to know?'

'I *couldn't*.' Andromeda was deeply shocked.

'Oh, yes, you could,' said Catherine, all smiling certainty.

'No! I'm such a bad liar.'

'But I am not,' retorted Catherine. 'You are my friend and if I choose to ask you to stay with us, no nosey little clerk need suggest to me that I pay you for the privilege.'

Andromeda looked hunted. 'Can I think about it?'

'No,' said Catherine. 'I need to know *now*.'

★ ★ ★

'Don't blame me if there's trouble,' said Dulcie Tims. 'And what does she call 'weekends'?'

'Friday evening to first thing Monday morning.'

'Those kids for five days on the trot!

54

They'd have to take you away in a plain van!'

'I can manage them.'

'And pigs have wings,' snorted Dulcie in black disbelief. 'They're spoiled rotten. Left for five minutes and they're all yelling their heads off. Good job I had that fried bread to shut 'em up.'

Andromeda preferred not to think of Catherine's reaction to the sight of her three greasy children and to Dulcie's stertorous instructions as she made the difficult three-point turn in order to descend the hill.

'You'll have trouble with that one, mark my words,' Dulcie said. 'She's got a tongue on her.'

'Never to me.'

'You'll see,' said Dulcie. 'When do you go?'

'We've got to get the room fixed up first. There's a lot of junk in it.'

'I'll bet . . . and damp as hell, I make no doubt.'

'Not Mrs Grant's garage room,' demurred Andromeda with conviction.

*   *   *

The room was not damp. Sunlight flooded in through two large windows. It did not take long to touch up the white walls and the timber floor was quickly covered by a large Chinese carpet.

'The pattern's good,' volunteered Catherine, 'as long as you don't look at the bald parts. Bloody moths.'

She unearthed a portable gas stove and gave it to Andromeda to clean. 'It will do for now, and I'll buy you a kettle. There are plenty of pots and pans and crockery over at the house.'

Cane furniture was unstacked, washed down, dried off and piled with cushions.

'I go in for tapestry when I am pregnant,' said Catherine, strewing more cushions around the floor. 'Don't dare tell me there are too many.'

In a fury of energy she dug up plants from the garden, potted them and hung them so that they trailed and made patterns against the bare walls. She rammed huge clumps of mother-in-law's-tongues and overgrown ficus into massive Chinese egg jars, skilfully concealing the chipped edges.

'This is your *own place*,' she said, decisive among the greenery.

'What on earth is going on here?' demanded Paul, materialising in the doorway and blocking the light.

★ ★ ★

'When I wanted you to have a nanny you refused.'

'Of course I did. I want a *girl*, not a nanny. I know all about *them*.'

She saw his lips tighten and did not care. If he was still stupid enough to feel intimidated by reference to her upper-class English background, that was his problem. She was in no way to blame for the accident of birth that he considered had rendered her unfairly privileged but to which she never gave a thought. She sometimes felt their relationship had never recovered from a remark at a party, overheard by both of them but acknowledged by neither, 'The difference between those two is that he is consciously classy and she has unconscious class.' She was forgiven neither her casual rejection of the mores of her kind nor the placid assurance of what he thought of as her 'vulgarities'. She was tired of playing down her natural behaviour and instincts in order to keep him good-tempered.

'She is just here to help out,' she now said roughly, 'not as a bloody status symbol.'

'That's obvious enough.'

To her surprise there was the trace of a smile, then he sighed and shook his head at her. 'If it's what you want — anything to keep you reasonable. Because you've been hell to live with lately.'

'Haven't I just!'

Her smile was brilliant but without humour.

'Well then . . . '

'Well . . . '

She was growing more assured by the minute. It was good to see how easily confusion could blur his smooth good looks.

'Someone will have to go and collect her bits and pieces.'

'Not me,' he said quickly. 'And don't dare take your car up there. You'd break an axle.'

She did not tell him of the deep scratches to the enamel of her car, nor of the new loud sound of the exhaust system. Sufficient unto the day.

'Well then . . . ' he said again, and actually kissed her before he left.

Before his car turned out of the drive she was dialling Janie Gordon's telephone number.

★   ★   ★

Janie sounded wary.

'I think we should meet,' stated Catherine without preamble. 'There is something I want to discuss with you.'

'What?'

The note of alarm was obvious.

'Nothing that can't wait. Could we have lunch one day next week? I could pick you up at your office on Tuesday.'

'Not Tuesday,' said Janie, too quickly.

'Wednesday? Thursday?'

'I don't know. I do have appointments.'

'But I presume you still eat. Shall we say Wednesday?'

There was the sound of a female voice in the background then an unconvincing ruffle of papers.

'I don't know . . . Are you sure you can't tell me what it's about?'

'Jan-ee!' said Catherine, 'I am up to my eyes in children as I am sure you are up to your eyes in work. I'd like a quiet lunch with you so that we can *talk*.'

The voice in the background grew louder.

'I'll pick you up in your foyer at twelve-thirty on Wednesday,' said Catherine, claiming attention.

'Maybe. But one o'clock would suit me better.'

Resistance was obviously crumbling.

'It wouldn't me,' said Catherine, 'and I'm sure you could push things round a bit if you tried. Look forward to seeing you.'

She hung up the phone before Janie had time to argue. Today it had to be triumph all the way.

6

It was almost one o'clock when Catherine, out of breath and out of temper, arrived in the colonnaded foyer of the building in which Janie had her office. A peacock throng of murmuring young men and women cluttered the marbled, mirrored precinct. She had to shove her way through them to where she could see Janie waiting, tight-lipped, beside the lift.

Damn it, she could at least have stood near the doors — even come out onto the *pavement*.

'I had given you up,' Janie said coldly, standing back to allow others to occupy the lift for which she had obviously rung and making no bones about showing resentment that now she could not take it with them.

'Don't start,' responded Catherine dangerously. 'I've been having one hell of a time. Why didn't you warn me about the parking? I was beginning to think that the only way to get rid of the car was to set fire to it.'

'You didn't ask. I could have easily arranged it for you.'

Such casual claim to have the ability to

solve a problem she had found so intractable was no more endearing than the equally casual elegance she had been unwise to forget was Janie's trademark. This meeting was getting off to a bad start.

Catherine took a deep, calculated, steadying breath. As well to remember that one was now called upon to be not only a manipulator but, if the cards ran badly, a supplicant. She slipped on bonhomie with smiling ease.

'No matter,' she said. 'We've made it. So don't let's start by fighting.'

'Fair enough,' retorted Janie. 'We'll leave it until it becomes clear what we have to fight about.'

All Catherine's ill-temper blew away in an explosion of laughter. She took Janie's bent and stiffly angled arm.

'Where do we eat? You will know the best place now.'

The best place was a brisk, downhill walk away. Janie, adroitly removing herself from all chumminess, did not appear to care that her longer stride took her well ahead of Catherine and that she could be easily lost among the plunge of office workers urgent for food. Catherine, accustomed to the relaxed pace of the Peninsula, fell behind. Bucketing comfortably along she was amused to see that on the other side of Macquarie Street, joggers

— avoiding any eye contact with passers-by — were forging onwards and upwards; they were all male and mostly ran alone. Their noontide determination, all pumping elbows and pounding of reinforced rubber soles, was endearing; the stupid buggers. Mindful of her own careful intake of the petrol-polluted air of the city, she preferred not to think of what lung-deep inhalation might be doing to them. She caught up with Janie down below The Rocks and above the water.

Sandstone buildings, buffed clean of the muck of years and consciously seductive with umbrellaed outdoor tables, puffed out the good scent of food. A quick glance inside showed the clever use of rafters, naked wood and old prints.

'Inside or out?' asked Janie.

Catherine blasted the stupidity of such an enquiry with a look.

'When did they do all this?'

'Some time ago.'

She had been so busy having children she had not had the time to notice that Sydney, too, had burgeoned.

Beneath the striped umbrella she received the menu as though it were Holy Writ. The service was quick.

'These prawns. This crab,' Catherine said in a low, ecstatic growl.

'I don't imagine you came just for the food.'

'No, but isn't it *good*?'

She ate slowly, with concentration. Enjoyment was so palpable that the tastebud might have been her own discovery.

'I wonder if you know,' she said dreamily, 'how appetite vanishes when one sits down to a meal for which one has shopped and then has prepared oneself? How such intimacy precludes enjoyment? But when food is *proffered* — when it comes with all the delight of anonymity — ah, the bliss!'

She was aware that she sounded affected, but did not care. If Janie did not recognise her truth there were plenty of women who would.

'Oh God, you haven't changed,' said Janie.

Catherine, aware of how deep and how grievous the change in herself, speared her crab.

'Knock it off, Catherine.' The tone was amiable, nevertheless notice was given that patience was short. 'What do you want?'

Catherine put down her fork, lifted her arms and spread them wide; the gesture needed more room than the proximity of other tables allowed.

'For the moment,' she replied, 'just to be here. Out! — enjoying the illusion of freedom and the rare pleasure of the company of a female friend.' Her satisfaction was excessive as she reached for the bottle of wine.

So you miss all the ones you dropped so carelessly when you married, do you? Janie thought wryly. And I bet you've been too uppity to join the local mothers' group. 'No!' she said, putting a firm hand over her own glass.

'Oh, come *on*! I can't drink it all.'

'You almost have.'

Catherine registered the level of the wine in the bottle with surprise. The last years had been so full of pregnancies and lactation that wine, spirits and cigarettes had all, perforce, been foresworn. She had thought the wholesome habits were ingrained. Barnaby was so lately weaned that she still refused wine at dinner, leaving Paul to drink alone and to grumble because, once opened, the bottle had to be drunk straightaway or left to spoil. He always chose heartburn in preference to waste.

'Did I drink all *that*?' she asked, greatly pleased.

'You did. Too many expense-account lunches have made me wary of midday excess.'

Catherine did not feel in the least wary. The light was so clear, the air so salt-fresh, and the conversations at near-by tables, on which she was shamelessly eavesdropping, were so full of hinted and delicious improprieties, that she felt quite giddy and light-hearted. Here was the world she had left behind and her appetite for it was as robust as for the squelchy, gorgeous, garlicky prawns. She mopped up the sauce with the crusty remains of her bread roll and cocked her head at Janie.

'You don't like me any more, do you?'

'I could always take you or leave you,' Janie lied.

Though he had not been mentioned, Paul was as potent between them as though sitting at the table in the spare chair that an ingratiating young man was now attempting to claim.

'But we *do* mind,' Catherine said so crisply that he flinched in alarm. 'What if the chair *is* empty? Our conversation is private. Would you wish to intrude upon *that*?'

She watched his crestfallen retreat with considerable satisfaction. When she returned her attention to Janie she found that her lunch companion was drinking from a full glass and that the bottle of wine was empty.

'I am merely saving you from yourself,' Janie said, with exasperated hauteur.

'That's better!' Catherine cried, beaming. 'Now, perhaps, we can *talk*!'

★ ★ ★

When she first attempted to contact Janie she had had no clear idea of what she wished to say; the impulse had been as instinctive as that of a non-swimmer flailing in deep water. In the week following Andromeda's arrival, when she found she could move from room to room, unimpeded by the constant presence of children, and could actually leave the house without having first to organise the wearing of nappies, shoes, sunhats, and the straps of car seats, she had felt bewildered. She had lost the ability to take the long, free stride. Then the idea had arrived like a bird taking sudden perch upon a tree. Its presence could not be ignored. It had laid an imperative upon her.

'Your agency,' she now said to Janie. 'We all know how successful it is. How about widening its scope?'

'It's wide enough for me.'

'Then you've stopped thinking. How would it be if you had not only a theatrical agency but a literary agency too? If you peddled both people and plays — maybe even books?'

66

'Words aren't my thing.'

'But they are mine.'

Before her marriage Catherine had been not only a successful features writer but had been within an ace of taking over the editorship of Australia's most glossy magazine. She willed Janie to remember that.

'So what?'

She was not remembering well enough.

'I can edit, rehash and advise. I know what the public wants and I know all the right people.'

'You did,' countered Janie. 'The world has turned.'

'And what makes you bloody well think I can't turn with it?'

It was a safe enough question; Janie did not have the facility for rudeness she herself enjoyed.

'I didn't mean that,' said Janie, obligingly.

'Then what do you mean?'

'I can hardly pass an opinion between one mouthful of rhum baba and the next. What made you order these things?'

'I remembered your sweet tooth — and your sweet nature.'

'Bollocks,' exclaimed Janie.

They were becoming more comfortable together by the minute.

'Do you realise what you're trying to do?' Janie asked. 'You are trying to muscle in on my business!'

'To our mutual advantage.'

'I don't know how you have the nerve!'

'Desperation,' Catherine said.

Janie's look was long and her consonants careful.

'Your desperation is my washpot, and over it I cast out my shoe.'

Catherine clicked her tongue. 'I'd love to see you when you go in for midday excess,' she said.

She knew that she was looking mussed and flushed, that the skin on her bare brown arms, which she now stretched across the table, was as dry and rucked as an unironed sheet, and that her imperfectly shaved armpits were revealed for public scrutiny. She knew that her face, lifted to the sun, showed lines around the eyes as deep as though scored by a scone-cutter.

'Janie, Janie,' she said, vulnerable, defenceless and crafty.

Janie looked away.

'You really should keep out of the sun,' she said.

'But it's the old Pommie lust. The disease of the deprived. One hint of golden warmth and there we are, flat on our backs and given to indecent exposure.'

'I thought the ladies in your garden-rooms wore hats.'

'Who told you that? Kipling? Betjeman? Paul?'

He could not long be kept from the cut and thrust.

'It's all to do with him, isn't it?' Janie said, snapping her fingers for the bill. 'But you must fight your own private war. Go home, Catherine.'

'I wonder,' Catherine said, aware that she was playing her last card, 'why I had formed the impression that it was *our* war?'

She had lost none of her old manipulative skills; she had wrung from the reluctant Janie permission to use her city address for correspondence and her telephone number for initial contact.

'Your girl can always say that I'm out and will ring back.'

'You don't know Eve, do you?' Janie had said.

Aha, thought Catherine, noting the twitch of the lip.

As they had plodded their way back up Macquarie Street, Janie had turned a morose eye on her. 'Now do something for me,' she said.

'Get rid of those damn trousers. They

look as though you got them at St Vincent's.'

'I did. It's the only place I have the nerve to shop these days. Imagine what Paul would say.'

Their sudden wild laughter had made heads turn.

As she took the swooping road home to the top of the plateau the memory of the conspiratorial amusement warmed her. The car windows were wide and the late afternoon breeze rising from the sea was clean and cool. Above her now was nothing but sky, and her hands on the wheel of the car looked brown and capable, the wedding ring hidden beneath the flat, soft spread of the peasant silver of too many other rings.

This day I have been added unto, she thought. No, she corrected herself, this day I have cast aside my mantles and — oh, God, I forgot to buy the veal.

An unexpected, and not wholly welcome, discovery was that Andromeda read cookery books as though they were novels and had a pronounced leaning towards haute cuisine. She had suggested that Swedish veal 'birds' would make a tasty dinner.

Barnaby, pink and bathed, his hair flat to his skull, was perched expectantly in his highchair. Jenny and Simon, in pyjamas, were crouched towards the television set.

'Mumm-ee!' they wailed as, with an accusing look at Andromeda, she switched it off.

'Did you get it?' Andromeda asked anxiously.

Catherine cast her bag from her. 'Never gave it a thought. I'll have to whip down to the village and pick up a cooked chook.'

Andromeda's lips were severe.

'There'll be time to do chips,'

Andromeda closed her eyes.

'All right! Straw potatoes then. And I'll do a sauce. And there will be *salad*!'

'It's nothing to do with me,' said Andromeda.

Too bloody right it isn't, Catherine fumed inwardly, marching back to the car.

As she swerved out of the drive she narrowly missed Paul's car swerving in. What was *he* doing home so early? The familiar vexations of home settled on her like stifling dust. Her mouth was dry as she drove to the village, all the while steeling herself for the evening ahead.

7

'What?' Catherine plucked Barnaby from the bath and planted him, dripping, on her hip, as she swung round to face her husband.

'Say that again!' she demanded.

'I forbid you,' Paul repeated, but with much less certainty than he used the first time.

Catherine gave a bray of angry laughter.

'Are you serious? Has the Victorian husband spoken? Come off it, Paul!'

'I will rephrase it then.' His voice was tight. 'I advise you, very strongly, to give up this mad idea.'

'I didn't ask for advice. I told you what I am going to do.'

'No, you're not,' he said. 'You most certainly are not.'

And left her.

Catherine polished Barnaby dry with an energy which brought squawls of protest. She comforted him remorsefully. Children always got the backlash of their parent's anger.

'My darling, my little love,' she crooned, clasping him to her and succeeded in comforting him not at all.

God, I seem to make a mess of everything, she groaned to herself, and, as if to prove the point, Andromeda arrived and announced there was no toilet paper in the downstairs loo and Mr Grant was being very cross about it.

'There are two full packets in the cupboard under the basin,' Catherine burst out. 'Do I have to think for everybody in this house?'

Andromeda's expression made it clear that thinking about toilet rolls came high in the duties of a good housewife and she departed at once to give help where she felt it was most needed.

He will be furious at having to mention such things to her, Catherine thought, but could not smile as she so often did at what she considered his maidenly refinements.

Barnaby strained away from her, his feet in her stomach and his head hung low so that he could see, upside down, the door through which Andromeda had left him. He stretched out his arms towards it in mute appeal and almost slipped from her grasp. She had to fight to get him upright and into his vest. Thank God the day was hot and all he needed now were nappy and pilchers.

He pulled at her empty breast as she lifted him.

'Sorry,' she said.

She had fed Jenny and Simon, the flow of milk copious and constant; she had had to struggle to be able to feed Barnaby at all. When he was only three months old she had given up, guilt-ridden and apologetic. It was another black mark against Paul; he should never have put her in the position of having to short-change a child.

You will have to stop this, she told herself; you snatch at every crumb to add to your poisoned cake of resentment. But she knew that she would not. Resenting Paul had become a way of life.

Last night, though, was all your own fault. You know well enough that when he comes home he is tired from the stresses of the day and it takes a strong drink and silent communication with the newspaper he has hitherto had no time to read before he is fit for human company.

And I came at him, as soon as he was sitting down with the paper, loud and ablaze with excitement. I was too enthusiastic to be willing to pussyfoot around. Pussyfooting never did come naturally, though, God knows, I have had to do a lot of it lately. The loss of a tight vagina and biddable bladder makes for careful footsteps. I took no care last night.

'I have been to the city,' I announced.

'The city?'

His patronising astonishment was a mistake, as was the quick look he flicked to see what I was wearing and the even quicker one which darted away from what he saw.

'I had lunch with Janie.'

He kept his attention on the paper but his left hand came up and, languidly, began to smooth his hair back. Only those who know him well are aware that the elegant gesture betrays tension.

'We are going into business together.'

'*What?*'

The paper was down and I had all his attention now.

We had had disagreements before but never a row of these proportions. I don't like to think of the things we both said. I didn't really mean half of them and can only hope he didn't either. In the middle of it all he suddenly leapt to his feet, and shaking his head and waving me away, hurried out of the room. A few minutes later I heard his car start. I knew how he felt. I would have given much to be able to turn my back on the ugliness too, but a mother cannot rush out of the house when things get too much. She has to stay, look after the children and get on with things.

I went to bed but did not sleep. I heard his car come back some time later but he did not come up to the bedroom.

It seemed that enmity was now established and the battle lines drawn.

It wasn't what I really wanted. But what *did* I really want?

Whatever it was, I realised that I came to Paul with a begging bowl that he would not or could not fill. I, Catherine, am no beggar.

Everyone has their own moment of truth; this was mine.

Halfway through the morning the telephone rang.

'Catherine,' Janie Gordon said, 'it's off.'

Rage was red and immediate. Bloody Paul!

'You've been got at!'

'If you mean I have been given the full details . . . '

'At great length, no doubt, in a voice throbbing with indignation and with a plea to you as a reasonable woman . . . '

'Something like that.' There was a touch of amusement in her voice — and a hint of complicity.

'Are you going to tell me what he said?'

'With pleasure. You have obviously taken leave of your senses; you had said no word to

76

him; the idea is preposterous; you find running the house and looking after the children beyond you so to entertain such an idea shows you have lost your grip on reality. Shall I go on?'

'No. I will. He complained about my lack of taste; that to approach you, of all people, showed an indelicacy he found offensive; that you . . . '

'That's enough,' Janie said crisply. 'When he got that far I told him to naff off. And you needn't laugh — I'm telling you to naff off too.'

Catherine's rage evaporated as quickly as it had risen.

'And so you should!'

Crisp Janie might sound but there was vulnerability in the air.

'I'm sorry. I should never have involved you. But you know me — act first, think later.'

'Yes . . . well . . . '

The lack of hostility was disarming. Catherine began to laugh.

'Between us we've made his day.'

'I don't find it funny. There is nothing more tedious to an outsider than the details of matrimonial squabbles.'

'This isn't squabbling, Janie, this is a full-on fight. And you are hardly an outsider.'

There was a silence at the other end of the wire.

'Hey!' Catherine said, but the machine had clicked.

As she got up she was confronted by Andromeda.

'I've put Barnaby down for his sleep and I'm taking Simon and Jenny to the beach. Do you think you can cope with him if he wakes?'

This is obviously my morning for rage, Catherine thought, stung by the touch of patronage in the girl's tone. Doesn't take long for the bloody meek to inherit the earth!

Since Andromeda had discovered she was a better cook than Catherine and that her years as an elder sister had given her an expertise in dealing with young children that Catherine had had no opportunity to acquire, her assurance had grown and, with it, a lively little sense of power. She tended to be clumsy with it and Catherine alternated between being amused and enraged.

'And there's a man at the door,' Andromeda was saying now.

'What does he want?'

'I didn't presume to ask him.'

Catherine's patience snapped.

'Well, presume now! Go and ask him!'

'Possums,' Andromeda said, returning and leaving in one fluid movement of affront.

Catherine stared at the man standing at the door.

'I know you!' she burst out.

The last time she had seen him he had been walking away showing too much sock.

She saw again the placid middle-aged face, the charitable mouth and easy smile and felt no embarrassment as she remembered their last encounter. She could see he remembered too. She liked the amused pleasure he could not conceal.

'Come in!' she cried. 'Oh, do come in!'

8

The man stepped inside and came to a halt.

She watched him look around, registering the cathedral vault of the ceiling, the wide, dramatic stone staircase, the gallery which ran along two sides of the house and the clean lines of the wooden railing over which one could look down on the black and white space of the hall.

'Beautiful,' he said.

Catherine immediately subtracted brownie points. Everybody said that.

He continued his careful inspection.

'But the children,' he went on, 'you must find it difficult with the children.'

The points were immediately restored.

'Come and sit down,' she insisted, and had difficulty in not taking his hand to lead him into the sunroom.

The garden lay stretched below — and the blue immensity of the pool. Beyond were the valley, the sands and the sea.

'Wonderful spot for watching the sun come up,' he said, sinking into the chair she indicated.

The glory of the rising sun went

unappreciated by Catherine, whose nights were, too often, mosaics of uneasy sleep and wakeful worry.

'How are you?' he asked. 'I have often wondered . . . '

'Fine,' she said hastily, 'just fine,' although she knew her appearance gave clear notice that she was not. 'Would you like some coffee?'

'No thank you.'

The conversation faltered. She felt awkward.

'Possums?' he prompted gently.

'Ah, yes!' she said and volubility took over.

She told him about the stained ceilings, the racket in the roof, the hoarse, unearthly cries of rage in the mango tree, the children's terror, the mutilation of her flowers and the vandalism of half-ripe fruit.

He listened.

'Do you have a tall ladder?' he asked.

She had. She told him where to find it.

'Then put your feet up and have a rest while I go and take a look.'

She not only put her feet up but dropped off into a doze. She woke to find him back in the chair and watching her.

'Oh!' she exclaimed. 'You should have woken me!'

'That would have been cruel,' he said

gently, further confusing her. 'People who fall asleep in the morning really need rest.'

She struggled to keep composure. 'What about the possums?'

'I've found two places where they are getting into the roof. You could discourage them. They don't like bright light, loud music or the smell of kerosene.'

'Are you serious? Are you suggesting I instal electric light and a radio in the roof?'

'Something like that.' He nodded cheerfully.

'I don't like loud music either. That's no answer. I just want the wretched things taken away.'

'I would have to bring cages.'

'Then bring them!'

He studied her face. 'Did you know that they are territorial animals and if I take them away and release them somewhere else, the possums there will attack them? They don't like invaders on their patch.'

'I know how they feel! And I don't much care. Possums have their problems. I have mine.'

'So you do,' he agreed.

He was still looking at her. 'You're English, aren't you?'

'How can you tell? My accent or my dislike of possums?'

'The possums,' he said. 'Definitely the possums.'

Was he laughing at her?

'Well . . . ' she said, bringing him back to the matter at hand.

'I'll get rid of them for you,' he said, as though comforting a child. 'Now, do you think I might have that coffee?'

When she came back with the tray he was settled in the large chair, which no longer looked so large.

'No children today?'

'The baby is asleep. The other two have been taken to the beach. I have a girl to help me.'

He looked around. 'With a house this size you need one.'

'There are *cleaners* of course.'

'Of course,' he echoed. 'I can't imagine you sweeping or scrubbing.'

'I polish!' she said, suspecting light mockery. Dead on her feet she might be but she always found energy to wax her beloved furniture.

'English eighteenth century. What can beat it?' His eyes on her were warm, amused, appreciative. 'Some people have the same sort of patina.'

He couldn't mean her, could he? Not in her present state!

She found herself hoping that he did.

She bent her head and busied herself with the pouring of the coffee.

'How is it?' she enquired, very much the polite hostess as she watched him sip.

'Just as I like it.'

The sound of him swallowing seemed alarmingly intimate.

They drank in silence.

'Well,' he said at last, putting his cup down and rising massively from the chair. 'I'll bring the cages tomorrow. About this time. Don't get up. I'll see myself out.'

When he had gone she sat and looked round at the soft gleam of cherished wood and shapes of abiding charm, but her pleasure was less than usual. He had left the room empty.

'The possum man has been,' she told Andromeda when she brought the children home.

'I know. That old chap who came as I was going out.'

'He's not old!'

'He must be fifty.'

The girl could be very irritating. And now was being more so.

'You are going down to the village, aren't you?' she was pressing. 'You won't forget this time, will you?'

'Forget what?'

'*The veal*! For the Swedish birds!'

Tonight was no night for haute cuisine. Paul's mood was such that he might not come home for dinner but eat in town.

'I'm not going to the village.'

'O-ooh!' she sounded in pain.

'There's no point. Mr Grant may not eat at home tonight — '

'But he *will*! I told him I was cooking something very special. He'll be here.'

Her confidence was enraging.

Catherine let her black temper show.

'Do you know what they do to those poor little calves to make your veal?' she asked savagely. 'I don't know how you can bear to buy it!'

'Oh, dear,' Andromeda said, 'is it worse than what they do to the little lambs then?'

Upstairs Barnaby woke and began to cry.

Andromeda began to move towards the staircase but Catherine barred her path.

'*I'll* get him,' she said.

Paul came home and was fed, not on Swedish birds, but a six-months-old curry from the deep freeze. Andromeda was mortified.

Paul took his indigestion to bed in the guest room and Catherine discovered that the luxury of having a bed to oneself might be pleasure but there was no happiness in it.

9

'If he comes looking for tea and sympathy, remind him he's three kids too late,' Eve Castle said tightly.

'What makes you think he'll come or that I have any sympathy to offer?' Janie Gordon replied.

Eve grunted.

'Don't try that on with me.'

Janie was not actually trying it on. She could not believe Paul would have the effrontery to show up and her emotions towards him were far from sympathetic. She had not liked his tone of voice when he had telephoned her to complain and then demand that she reject any plans she might have to let Catherine join her in business. It was not out of concern for him that she had turned Catherine down but because she refused to be drawn into a distasteful situation. After she had ended her conversation with Catherine she had felt an urgent need to cleanse herself, like a cat, licking long and devotedly, washing coat, paws and ears over and over again.

'I know you,' Eve was saying.

'I want nothing more to do with him.'

'I would. If I were you,' Eve added, 'I'd like the chance to get back at him for what he did. But you, you don't seem to think he's got anything to pay for and you'll let him get away with it.'

'Get away with what? He can't be blamed for finding he liked somebody better than me. I've done it myself. I was engaged when I met Paul.'

'There we are then,' Eve said triumphantly. 'Another black mark against him. But for him you'd probably be married now, with kids.'

'And probably very miserable. I was lucky to find out I didn't love Dan enough.'

'Oh, God,' exclaimed Eve, in disgust. She always became disgusted when love was mentioned.

And with good reason, Janie thought. I'm hardly an advertisement for the joy of it.

'I need time off,' Eve said now. 'The chemotherapy is knocking my sister around. I don't like her being on her own so much.'

Intentional or not, the point was made. Paul was relegated to the unimportant.

'Of course,' Janie said.

When she arrived home his car was in her drive and she could not put hers into the garage.

'I thought we might take yours and go and have a bite to eat,' he cut in, to counter her anger. He was shower-fresh and fragrant as he bent to her window. And much good will that do you! She thought cynically.

'No!'

'Oh, yes.'

'No!'

'Then I must blow my horn until . . . '

He would, too. She knew him. She also knew her neighbours. They had opinions about women who lived on their own.

'Get in,' she said, black hate in her voice.

He locked his own car and slid in beside her.

'We'll go to Sherman's,' he told her. 'The food's good and the parking is easy.'

He was unbelievable. They always used to go to Sherman's.

She drove without looking at or speaking to him. He shrugged his shoulders and sat with arms folded, watching the road.

She snaked around the leafy bends of her suburb, came out on the main road and headed north.

'This isn't the way,' he said.

'We're not going to Sherman's.'

'Hornsby!' he said incredulously. 'Do people *eat* in Hornsby?'

'They do in Gosford,' she responded, swinging left on the highway. 'And New-castle.'

'They're miles away! Are you mad?'

She was. She was lunatic with anger.

'We could turn off to Berowra Waters,' he said. 'The food there is very good.'

She did not turn off for Berowra Waters.

Miles on she took the Peats Ridge turn. It was dark now.

'What the hell . . . ?' he said. 'Look, Janie. Stop the car. I just want to talk to you.'

'But I don't want to talk to you.'

'You're being childish!'

'You bet I am.'

She waited until they were on a long, straight stretch of road with no house lights in sight.

'Damn,' she muttered. 'This thing is overheating. I'll have to pull up.'

'Good,' he said.

She slid the car to a halt by the side of the road and cut the engine. He turned towards her. 'Now . . . ' he said.

'For God's sake, Paul. At least open the bonnet.'

She reached for the torch she carried in the door pocket. 'Here's a cloth too.'

She pressed both on him. 'Be careful when you open the radiator. You could easily get scalded.'

She waited until he was out of the car with the door slammed shut and then started the engine. The car leapt away. She drove some way down the unlit road, did a U-turn, came back, and tooted as she streaked past him and headed for home.

The night was black now. Who would be unwise enough to stop for a man suddenly appearing in their headlights and waving his arms?

Eve will be proud of me, she laughed to herself, out on the highway again, her foot down hard. And I wonder what Catherine would say?

Will say, she corrected herself, for she knew she would be unable to resist telling her. She did not bother to examine her motives, they were too complex; for the moment she was content to enjoy her moment of wicked satisfaction.

When she arrived home she squeezed past his car, went in and rang the NRMA.

'A friend has left his car in my drive but I've forgotten where he said he'd hide his keys and I can't get my car into the garage. Could you help?'

The van arrived within minutes and in no time at all Paul's car was out on the road and hers safely locked away.

'Thank you so much,' she said, as fervently as though she had been plucked from danger, and pressed a tip on the surprised young man.

'Goodnight. Sleep well,' he said and went away shaking his head at her great burst of sudden laughter.

★ ★ ★

She was robbed of her pleasure in telling Catherine.

Paul was carrying his mobile phone.

'Come and get me, Cat,' he said. 'I'm on the road to Wisemans Ferry.'

'What on earth are you doing there?'

'Never mind.'

'But I do mind. Why are you out there at this time of night and how can I leave the children?'

'What's Andromeda for?'

'Has your car broken down?'

'For God's sake!' he cried. 'Just come and get me.'

'You know I'm a bad night driver.'

'Just get here. I'll drive back.'

'But what about your car?'

'Forget about the bloody car,' he said savagely. 'Just come and get me.'

'But what have you done with it? Where is it?'

He ground his teeth. 'It's in Janie's drive, if you must know.'

91

Catherine fell silent.

'Well?'

'Then tell her to collect you,' she said and put the phone down.

It rang again, repeatedly, but she did not answer it.

★ ★ ★

A reckless slug of whisky gave her a good night's sleep and she was sitting in the chair in the sunroom taking an unaccustomed look at the way the colours of sea, sky and land change as the sun rises from the sea, when his car wheels scattered the gravel in the drive. He went straight to his bathroom and she heard the shower water begin to run. It ran for a long time. Wasteful, she thought irritably. He did not take breakfast but left again before the clock struck eight. The children slept on. Andromeda appeared. 'Can I make you some coffee?'

'I'll show you how,' Catherine said hastily. 'I've chucked out that muck you brought here the other day.'

Andromeda went in for instant coffee and enhanced it with coffee whitener. The very sight of it made Catherine, who was a coffee purist, want to throw up. 'The coffee is in the container with the wooden lid, on the second shelf of the cupboard by the window. The filter papers are beside it.'

'Filter papers?' Andromeda echoed blankly.

The coffee was brewing when the telephone rang.

'Good morning,' chirped Janie Gordon.

Catherine looked at her watch.

'My word, you must have been up all night,' she said with heavy innuendo.

'I actually slept well,' Janie said equably.

Catherine's voice grew even sharper. 'I hope you're not expecting thanks.'

'What for?'

'Don't be stupid! For delivering him home, of course!'

'Delivering him home! What are you talking about? I dumped him!'

Catherine felt her jaw actually drop. It was not just a writer's way of indicating surprise, then. 'Jane-ee-ee?' she managed to say.

Janie's voice was crisp.

'Your husband arrived at my place and suggested we go to Sherman's for something to eat — and to talk. I didn't think much of the idea. So I drove him out into the country and left him there.'

'You didn't!'

'I did.'

'So that was why he rang me on his mobile and asked me to collect him.'

'And what did you say?'

'I told him to ask you.'

There was a small silence and then they both began to splutter with laughter. Once started they could not stop.

'He didn't get back till nearly daylight,' Janie said. 'The taxi driver wanted cash and he didn't have enough on him. Their arguing woke me. I had to go down and bail him out.'

'Poor Paul.'

'Poor Paul.'

Catherine wiped her eyes and liked to think Janie was wiping hers.

'Have lunch with me,' she said impulsively.

'No way!'

'Oh, go on!'

'No!'

'Same place?'

'No!'

'Same time. I'll meet you there next Wednesday.' She rang off before Janie could say more. She'll be there, she thought jubilantly.

Then reality started to roar in like an express train.

What is happening to my life? she wondered in sudden panic.

My relationship with Paul may not be ideal but we are in a *marriage*.

Marriage gives life a framework and offers

the promise of safety. What if the framework crumbles? Where do I find safety then?

Scoring points suddenly began to seem a very juvenile way of conducting a serious business.

But then, she castigated herself, what am I but juvenile?

10

Barnaby wakened early. Catherine, who was sitting watching the dawn break, got up, collected him and brought him to sit with her. He did not wish to sit. He clambered about awkwardly, feet pummelling her stomach, fiddled with her hair, explored her face with his fingers and farted loudly into his nappy. In self-defence she hoisted him away into the bathroom and ran the water. The sound woke Jenny and Simon. Suddenly the bathroom was full of boisterous children. Andromeda arrived and imposed order.

At breakfast cereal bowls were overturned, food spat out and spoons used as weapons. Andromeda had to impose order again.

After breakfast Jenny and Simon teased Barnaby, confined behind the bars of his playpen. They squealed; he roared with frustration. It all ended in tears, Catherine's included. There was no peace until Andromeda took the older two away to the beach and the tear-streaked baby slept.

And the possum man was coming.

He will not think I have patina today, Catherine grimaced, inspecting her face, pinched with her miseries.

He did not say it, but his eyes did. She was grateful to him for that.

'I've brought three cages. I know where to put them.'

She left him to it.

She was considering a restorative gin and tonic when he reappeared.

'All done. But be prepared for a racket. They hate being caged.'

'They only come out at night! We'll be asleep.'

'They'll wake you, but I'm sure your husband will be able to deal with them. Call me when you've caught them.'

'Oh, dear,' she sighed, knowing how Paul would react. She bit her lip. She could not let this damn man see her in tears again.

He stood looking at her.

'You're having a real tough time, aren't you?' he said.

He did see her in tears again.

'Tell you what,' he suggested, 'if you don't mind, how about you sitting down and letting me make *you* some coffee?'

It would take more than bloody coffee!

Her tears turned to sobs.

'Now, now,' he said, and put his arms around her.

She sank against him. It was like falling

into a deep feather bed. Paul was fit and hard-muscled. He would not give houseroom to an ounce of fat. His lean body enabled him to wear clothes well but his hipbones had a cutting edge. She was in no danger of damage now.

Her sobs turned into tremulous laughter.

'What?' he asked, putting her away from him and bending his face to hers.

She had difficulty in not holding up her face to be kissed better and throwing herself back into his arms.

She made the coffee. He could not be allowed to think her totally useless.

He looked at her over the rim of his cup.

'You ought to be drinking Guinness, not coffee. It would do you good. And at a guess,' he added, 'you probably need vitamin B pills.'

'I've got them. I forget to take them.'

'That figures. When you get really low it's too much trouble to try to get better.'

'You know about that?'

'You bet I do.'

They smiled a long smile at each other.

It had seemed only polite to try to look as good as she could when a stranger came to the house but all she had been able to do was to put a soft lilac eye shadow on her lids to make her eyes look greener. Her shirt showed a patch of damp where she had wiped away some of Barnaby's breakfast cereal and she was glad she was sitting on a cane chair or another patch of damp would have been visible.

'You must think me an awful mess,' she said. 'I wasn't always like this.'

'What were you like?'

It was impossible to take offence. His easy question was full of genuine interest and his pleasant face was kind.

'Good at everything I did,' she answered recklessly. 'Golden Girl, that was me. It all lay before me. I knew everybody. I had a future.'

'As what?'

'Writer. Editor. Mover and shaker.'

'And that was what you wanted?'

'Yes! I wanted to do what I enjoyed doing in the biggest way possible and earn all the kudos I could get.'

'And did you?'

'Not quite. Something came up. Nature is very cunning. I began to hear the biological clock ticking. I wanted a marriage and children too.'

'In fact you wanted everything.'

'You bet,' she admitted. 'Of course I did! Why not?'

'Why not indeed?'

He was lying back in his chair, legs crossed, holding his coffee cup balanced on the rising curve of his stomach. He had been very dark when he was younger. His jowls were still dark but his hair was greying. The light shining in his eyes made them the colour of dark sherry. His bulk filled the chair. Comfortable. She was very aware of him and quite unprepared for the directness of his next question.

'When you say you wanted children — whose children did you want?'

'I don't know what you mean.'

'Think about it.'

He watched her.

'Paul and I were both ready for marriage,' she said defensively. 'We both wanted children.'

'How important was it that they should be *his*?'

'Stop right there,' she blazed.

He did, but he did not take his eyes from her face.

When she met them her hostility crumbled. His concern was too powerful to resist.

It was luxury to talk. To spill it all out.

'We made a good pair,' she continued. 'Two successful career-minded people deciding that the time had come. I was a good wife. A credit to him. I didn't see why I shouldn't be a good mother. I'd had no experience with children but I expected it would come naturally with one's own. I read everything I could. I did everything I should. I had a very easy first pregnancy and birth. Paul adored his little daughter. A whole new world opened up. I was all set to do well again. I was not prepared for the anxiety.'

'Anxiety?'

'She was so precious. What if we lost her? I hardly dared sleep. I infected Paul with my fear. We decided we must have another child . . . in case. I had no trouble with that pregnancy either — and the fear seemed to have left me but as soon as he was born it came back. Now there were two of them to worry about, I was terrified of cot death, of my milk drying up, of other people's germs, radiation, polluted water and what I would do if there were landslides, tidal waves or earthquakes. God, I was a mess.'

'So why did you have another child?'

'Not by choice, I can assure you.'

She thought back to the time she had discovered she was pregnant again. The shocked disbelief then the quiet nightmare. The sickly pregnancy, the children who whined because their mother could not cope, Paul's martyred good behaviour, the dreadful birth, the slow recovery that never came to an end and a relationship that seemed as though it must.

She sat hunched, her thoughts teeming.

The trouble is we went into marriage separately, each for our own reasons. There was love in it of course, we were each a *person* — and equals — but it became very unequal. Paul did not pee himself in public because he had become a father; the skin of his belly did not hang in folds because it had been stretched so much and so often it had lost all elasticity. Nothing in becoming a father had robbed him of his vitality or given him an understanding of what it might be like if it had.

'It's so unfair,' she burst out. 'We are *both* parents but his body isn't wrecked and he still has all his energy — and me! I hardly recognise myself — bloated, sagging, exhausted beyond belief . . . '

'No wonder. Having three children in three years must be like a jogger trying to run the four-minute mile.'

'Paul doesn't see it that way. He was used to my being efficient. Why can't I be efficient now? When he looks at me I can see him thinking 'Is this the woman I married?' '

'And are you?'

'I could be — if I was doing the things I'm naturally good at.'

'Do you wish you didn't have the children?'

'That's unfair!'

'It is, isn't it?'

He was unfazed by her flash of temper.

She subsided into moody silence.

'I see you have a nanny,' he began.

'A *girl*,' she corrected him. 'I have a girl to help me out. I don't abrogate my responsibilities no matter how inept I may be.'

And pompous, she thought, disliking herself more by the minute.

'Good for you.'

He was so placidly, so comfortably non-judgmental.

'I tried to get back, to find a way to be my old self again,' she found herself saying, and out it all came — the approach to Janie, the meeting, the agreement. 'And then it all fell down,' she said, but did not tell him how.

'You must have been desperate to have had such a crackpot idea,' he said.

He could certainly be judgmental when he tried!

He put a finger under her downcast chin and lifted it.

'The first thing you have to do is to get really well again,' he said gently. 'Now, what about your diet? Exercise? Deep breathing? Yoga? All those things?'

'I know all about *them*,' she scoffed.

'And another thing. This house. Do you *have* to live here?'

'Whatever do you mean?'

'Well ... ' he said, looking around disparagingly, 'stone floors, stone staircases, bloody great pool — you must live on your nerves. You need a house on one level with French windows and a big, safe garden where you can turn the children loose but still be able to keep your eye on them ... '

'Paul would never sell this house! It's his status symbol. It impresses his clients. We entertain here — well, we used to.'

'Then why not rent it out until the children are off your hands? Some high-flyer would love it. Then you could rent somewhere more suitable.'

'Paul wouldn't ... '

'How do you know? Have you suggested it?'

'Hang on a minute,' she said, pulling herself together. 'You came here to get rid of my possums, not to reorganise my life.'

'So I did! What do you know?'

He was annoyingly unfazed.

'I don't even know your name!'

'Henry,' he said, 'Henry Green.'

'Well, Henry,' she said, indicating the conversation was at an end.

He rose to his feet at once.

'Tell your husband to keep his hands away from the animals. They'll be frightened and a possum scratch can be very nasty.'

She would do no such thing. Paul had thought it of little account when she was scratched, so let him take potluck.

'Are you married?' she asked suddenly.

'My wife is dead.'

The bleakness of his reply jolted her.

'I'm sorry,' she said, 'I didn't mean to . . . '

His hand on her shoulder was valedictory. 'I know you didn't, Mrs Grant.'

'Catherine.'

'Goodbye — Catherine.'

*   *   *

After he had gone she felt strangely elated. It was a long time since she had had such an intimate conversation with a man — or one so direct and positive with anybody, come to think of it.

He is quite right, I must get fit again as soon as possible. I know the food I should eat, the vitamins and minerals I should take and as far as yoga — I used to be there ohming with the best. I know the breathing — *and* the Chinese stomach muscle contractions — *and* how to strengthen the muscles of the pelvic floor. You can do those exercises while sitting at traffic lights or waiting in the Post Office queue. I can't see them enabling me to puff a cigarette vaginally like the girls I've heard met the boats at Port Said but then I'm not planning to meet any boats.

And as for Paul, it's a case of 'Once more into the breach.' I will do my best, I really will. He will not know I know about the comeuppance Janie handed out to him. He need never know. And I will not ask him why his car was in Janie's drive and he was stranded out in the sticks. My silence will be dignified. I will be pleasant. Glad to see him home. Considerate even. A wife who greets her warrior lord at the end of the day offering balm for his weariness after he has done battle on her behalf.

She suddenly realised she had not asked Henry Green where he had put the traps.

A hurried reccy revealed that two were on the top balcony beneath the spot where there were signs of entry into the roof and the third was fixed in the branches of the mango tree, which overhung the children's bedroom window. Then, full of good humour and good intentions, she went down to the village and bought the veal for Andromeda's 'Swedish birds'.

'They need Marsala, you know,' Andromeda said.

They got it. And snow peas, small, whole onions, mushrooms and tiny potatoes.

'I'll glaze them with honey and curry powder and grated orange rind.' Andromeda was rapt. 'And some lemon butter sauce would be nice.'

'Wouldn't it just!' Catherine said.

11

Paul came home. One hurdle down. She had been afraid he might not.

The meal was beautifully cooked. Andromeda bore her tray away to her room, casting anxious backward glances at Catherine, who was being liberal with black pepper.

She did not eat with them. Egalitarianism was one thing, social ease another — even Catherine recognised that.

Paul was quiet and guarded and seemed as glad as she was to have a little domestic peace. She let him finish his meal. A time of appreciative repletion seemed as good a way as any to bring up the question of selling the house.

'No!' he said. 'No!' and 'No!' again, only louder.

Her judgment had been lamentably faulty.

Was she mad? he demanded. This house was all they could ever want. Look at the number of times it had been photographed for magazines! It was the house everybody wished they had. And she had it. He had provided it for her. How could she be so graceless?

'It is no house for children,' she insisted.

'It's no house for bloody cardboard boxes all over the hall either!'

She shifted her tack.

'Do you know how many children die each year in backyard pools? Most pools are two metres deep — ours is six.'

'And very well fenced.'

'Are you here all the time to see the gate is not left open?'

The argument had gone back and forwards like a ping-pong ball.

While they were drawing breath they heard the rattle of metal and a loud slam.

'What was that?'

'It must be one of the traps.'

'What traps?'

'The possum traps. You'd better go and bring it down; the man will collect it in the morning.'

'What man?'

'The one you should have got in, but didn't.'

He shot her a venomous look and rushed out into the hall, kicking aside the cardboard boxes at the foot of the stairs.

She gathered them together and stacked them ready for replacement. It does look rather like the back room of a supermarket, she conceded.

He soon came down carrying a trap containing a big possum with a baby on its back. It was terrified and left a trail of poo all the way down the stairs.

Fortunately the pellets were hard and she was able to brush them hastily over the side with her handkerchief. No point in enraging Paul further. 'I've left a blanket for you to put over the cage,' she called after him.

When he came back indoors he brushed past her and went straight upstairs.

She was still willing to do her best so she followed him up and met him coming out of their bedroom carrying a bundle of his clothing and heading for the guest bedroom.

He obviously intended to prolong his stay there.

'There's no need for *this*,' she said, winsome and reasonable.

'I sleep better alone,' he said tightly. 'I'm sure you must.'

She did, but when sleeping better was more important than sleeping beside one's loved one, what did that say about the marriage?

'Goodnight then,' she said.

'Goodnight.'

It was as though they had said goodbye.

★ ★ ★

It was Andromeda's night for her weekly visit.

'She's got no sense, your Missis 'igh-and-mighty,' Dulcie Tims declared.

She had grown fond of Andromeda and resented Catherine for depriving her of the girl's company for the greater part of the week.

'We-ell,' Andromeda said forgivingly, 'she's English.'

While her devotion to Catherine remained unimpaired she was no longer in awe of her and felt quite able to regale Dulcie with tales of her failures and foibles without feeling the guilt of betrayal, for she was sure they would be found as endearing as they were to her. There was nothing whimsical about Dulcie. 'Cracked,' she muttered.

They were sitting in Andromeda's room.

'I'll never be able to get up again, you know that,' Dulcie grumbled, lowering herself gingerly onto the floor.

'Well, go on then,' she said, collapsing like a blancmange.

'*Well*,' Andromeda said, taking a deep breath. 'After dinner I brought my tray down from my room to the kitchen, just to see if it was all clean and tidy.' She did not say 'my' kitchen but the inference was plain.

'I thought you were supposed to look after kids, not kitchens.'

'We-ell,' she plucked at the blue slub-linen dress she was wearing.

'She gave me this. And . . . ' she pointed to her hair, 'she paid for me to have this done.'

The cut was short and saucy. As she moved her head around to demonstrate it, the light caught the new streaks of gold.

'I couldn't make out what was different about you,' Dulcie said with grudging approval and then, 'God Almighty! what have you got on your eyes?'

Andromeda leant forward conspiratorially. 'You put mascara on your lashes, see, and you crimp them with this little thing she gave me — it makes them curl up.'

Dulcie sighed heavily. 'Her and her mascara . . . '

'Oh, she doesn't wear any! She doesn't have to. She's got lovely eyelashes. Like a camel's.'

Dulcie snorted. 'Better not let her hear you say that.'

'I told her. She knew what I meant. She was pleased. And she said I made her laugh. I was an original.'

'And thank heaven for that,' Dulcie said. 'I couldn't be doin' with more than one of you around. Well . . . go on.'

'Ah, yes,' Andromeda said, and warmed to her tale. 'I was in the kitchen and they were out in the entrance hall. I don't know what gets into her sometimes. She keeps piling boxes at the bottom of that staircase so the kids won't try and climb up. She says it's dangerous.

'Well, it is — it's a stone staircase and one side of it curves round against the wall but the other side is open, no railings or anything. Railings would spoil the look. She certainly spoils the look — you should have seen the pile of cardboard boxes — there were even some of those white polystyrene ones the fruit comes in. Even then she's not satisfied. She stacks a couple of chairs outside their bedroom door so they can't crawl out and fall down.'

'She's not as daft as all that,' Dulcie conceded.

'Well . . . he says, 'Do we have to have this, Catherine?' all cold, and she says, 'We certainly do. If you don't like it we could always sell the house and buy one less likely to kill the children.' That started it. They didn't yell or anything — they were probably frightened of waking the kids — but they went at it hammer and tongs. They heard me in the kitchen and shut up. Then there was this noise. It sounded like a gun going off but she said it must be one of the traps. 'What traps?' he said. 'The possum traps, I forgot to tell you,' she says.

'So up they go and find which one has gone off and down they come with the cage with this possum inside. It had a baby on its back. They've got lovely eyes, haven't they, possums? She said to put a blanket over the cage and put it out for the man to collect in the morning. 'What man?' he said.

' 'The possum man, of course,' she said, 'the one you should have got but didn't.' '

'He comes tramping through the kitchen carrying the cage. The poor little possum must have been frightened out of its wits — it was pooping all the way. Then, when he sees me, he half hesitates, gives a bit of a smile and says, 'Nice meal, Andromeda. Well done.' You could have knocked me down with a feather.'

'Well,' said Dulcie, 'is that it?'

'Isn't it enough? What if they sell the house? What will happen to me?'

'You'll be all right,' Dulcie said with heavy humour. 'You've wormed your way in. They can't do without you now. You're indispensible.'

Andromeda thought about it. It didn't take long.

'I suppose I am,' she smiled, with modest pride.

12

The next morning Catherine awoke to the good smell of coffee.

It was half past eight.

Panicked, she leaped from the bed, struggled into her dressing-gown and rushed downstairs.

In the kitchen, Barnaby, safely hanging in his bouncer in the doorway, was bobbing up and down like a contented little cork. Jenny and Simon were sitting on the draining boards each side of the sink, over which Andromeda, her head held back and her thumb and finger curved at her lips, was blowing a perfect soap bubble.

It grew slowly, tremulously, fragile and glistening, delicately rainbow coloured. The children were holding their breath. Andromeda gently set it free and it floated slowly out towards the open window, where the breeze took it and it became invisible against the sky.

'More!' the children demanded.

'Where did you . . . ? I overslept . . . When did Mr Grant . . . ?' Catherine found herself babbling.

'Me Mum taught me. You must have

needed your sleep and I gave him scrambled egg,' Andromeda replied. 'A pinch of curry powder livens it up heaps.'

Her culinary tip was not well received.

'Bugger,' Catherine said, annoyed with herself for giving Paul such a plain example of how bad a wife and mother she could be.

'I'm sorry,' she said to Andromeda, 'and thank you for taking charge so well.'

'Oh, and he had a call, early on. His dad is real bad.'

'Not again!'

Oh, please, God, she thought, not another heart attack! How many can an old man survive?

'He said to make sure this week's shirts went to the laundrette and the others were picked up, and to get Jenny and Simon ready for half past three. He's leaving the office early and taking them up there.'

'Up there' was Leura in the Blue Mountains, three to four hours' drive away.

'I must ring him,' Catherine said, heading for the phone.

'He was going straight into a meeting. Better leave it for now.'

Catherine controlled herself with difficulty. 'I'll get dressed then,' she said.

No point in taking umbrage, she told herself, the girl is only doing her best. The

116

trouble is her best seems a damn sight better than mine.

★ ★ ★

When she finally spoke to Paul he was terse.

'Another attack,' he said. 'Bad one. Beth is insisting on nursing him at home. She wants him to see the children — in case — so have them ready.'

'How long will you stay?'

'How do I know? Remind Andromeda about the shirts. And, oh, I'll have to take your car because of the seats for the children. Get her to clean it up a bit — get rid of the wrappers and fruit-drink cartons and give it a wipe-round inside.'

'Anything else?' she asked heavily.

'Yes. Don't forget about that poor animal. It will be hungry and thirsty.'

She would not forget about the animal.

She would not forget, either, that he had not asked her if she would like to go too. She was fond of his parents, Beth and Ned. She liked their serenity and good sense and was amused by the interested way they observed Paul's upward mobility, congratulated him wholeheartedly on his successes but were neither boastful to others about them nor intimidated by them. Peter, their other son, was a conservationist, a worried man, and, she suspected, homosexual. Did they ever wonder how they came to have two such disparate sons? Not for the first time she thought how much more likeable they were than their progeny.

'I'll ring Beth now,' she said.

'No. The doctor will be there. Leave it till this evening.'

Instructions on what she should or should not do were rife.

'I'd like to see Ned too,' she said impulsively. 'I could follow you with Barnaby. I know there isn't room in the house for all of us but I could stay at the local hotel.'

'For God's sake,' he burst out. 'It isn't a party! The last thing Beth needs is to have people milling around.'

'But how will you manage the children without me? And how will they be? We've never been separated since they were born.'

'Here we go!' he said. 'Just what I might have expected. Can we cut out the fuss, Cat? Just get the children's things ready and try to be of some help for once.'

That was fighting talk but she had the good sense — for once — not to strike back. She rang off.

She dialled the Leura number straightaway.

'I'm so glad you called,' Beth said. 'The doctor's just gone. No, it isn't a heart attack — it's a stroke. Fairly bad but it can be coped with.'

She sounded brisk and sensible. 'What time do you expect to arrive?'

'Well,' Catherine said, her mind working fast. 'Paul is leaving with the children about half past three . . . '

'And you?'

'We didn't want to crowd you. Let's see how things go. I could come up later.'

'I wanted him to see the children while he can still — and maybe they'll remember him.'

At their age Catherine thought it unlikely, but did not say so.

'He's a good man to remember,' she said. And I wish Paul were more like him, she thought, but did not say that either. 'Is he . . . I mean . . . will he?'

'Who can say?'

'And how are you?'

'Coping.'

She would be too.

'You know I'm here if you want me,' Catherine said, her voice warm.

'I do. And I might. Bless you, girl.'

★   ★   ★

119

She turned away from the phone blinded with tears.

The death of a parent is a milestone in one's life. She remembered her sense of spinning loose, her safe tether gone, when her own father died. Her mother was just an absence — something other girls had but she did not. She had died in childbirth, leaving her daughter nothing to remember her by.

How was Paul feeling? However it was, he had made it plain it was something he did not wish to share with her. Could not? she wondered. Am I barren land to him, a place of no sustenance? And how high-falutin' can you get? No. Paul is not a sharer. And that is all there is to it.

'That man's here about the possums,' Andromeda announced, appearing with Barnaby in her arms and Jenny and Simon anchored to each side of her. They all stood and stared at her, dismayed by her tears. She stared back, piercingly aware of their togetherness, their peacefulness in each other's company. She had never felt so unwanted in her life.

'Show him where the cage is and tell him to take it away,' she replied.

She did not feel up to facing Henry Green today.

'Right,' Andromeda said, and they all

turned like a school of fish and left her.

As bad days went it was shaping up to be a corker.

Henry Green collected the cage and went.

He might have asked to see me, she thought petulantly.

★ ★ ★

So many of the children's good things were dirty.

The washer and dryer hummed. Suitcases were crammed, temperature can change rapidly. You always want the things you haven't brought. And I mustn't forget Jenny's Miss Piggy doll or Simon's kettle. Simon refused to leave the house without his little tin kettle. '*Ke-kull*!' he would scream as they went through the door. What else would they need to make them feel safe?

'Good God,' Paul exclaimed when he saw the suitcases and carrier bags, but had the sense to leave it at that. She did not tell him she had spoken to Beth.

'Are my shirts here?'

'No, but they are ready to be picked up. You have to drive past the shop. They know you are coming.'

She felt she had done as much as could be expected of her by organising the pick-up.

What time had she had to go down to the village?

His lips tightened. 'And the possum?'

'Gone.'

He seemed to feel that at least that was one worry less.

'Good,' he said to Andromeda when he inspected the inside of the car. 'Thank heaven for that. Good girl.' His tone was almost warm.

In silence Catherine helped him to stow the luggage in the car and fasten the children into their seats. Simon had to be packed around with cushions. Neither of them appeared upset when Paul, not she, climbed into the driver's seat. She choked back the ready tears as she waved them goodbye. They waved back enthusiastically, their little faces beaming.

'I'll make you a cup of tea,' Andromeda said.

'No. It's Friday. Almost time for you to be off.'

She took Barnaby from her. 'You might as well go a bit earlier. We'll be all right.'

She buried her face in Barnaby's sweet-smelling little neck to show how all right they would be. He clutched her hair and tugged and made pleased and pleasant noises.

As she moved towards the house she was aware that Andromeda, walking to her own room over the garage, was casting backward glances and frowning. She clutched Barnaby more tightly and her step quickened.

'Off you go!' she called, waving, and not looking back.

She brought his cot into her room and placed it beside the bed. Then she took him down to the kitchen and sat him in his chair while she prepared his food. He sang and banged his spoon while he was waiting, then began to pick at the knot of his bib. He worked with total concentration until it loosened and the bib fell to the floor. He smiled delightedly. She picked up the bib and tied it back on again. They grinned at each other and he attacked the knot again.

He was hungry and ate and drank devotedly. She bathed him, enjoying the pleasure of having the time to play with him. When he was ready for sleep she went to bed too and held his hand between the cot bars. He was the first to let go and roll over. She fell asleep almost immediately after-wards.

She did not hear the possum cages slam shut in the night, or the angry, incessant assault on the confining metal. She slept deep and sound. Her dreams were sweet. She was making pancakes for the children; soap bubbles were floating around their tousled heads; and she was expecting Henry Green. She was smiling.

13

The house was silent. She worked peacefully, putting away clothing, tidying cupboards, emptying vases of half-dead flowers and plumping up cushions. She wheeled Barnaby in his play-chair from room to room as she worked and they talked at each other, exchanging small, meaningful noises and pulling funny faces. Time lapped around her tranquilly; she was used to it rushing her along with the force of foaming water. If only, she thought. She went over it all yet again. She was sick of it but there was no escape.

She had been so happy when she was pregnant with Jenny — so well. She had revelled in this new adventure. The birth was no more difficult than first births usually are and she had been pleased with herself for a job well done. The last thing she expected was that she — so blithe, so confident — would become prey to such appalling fears. She hardly dared sleep. She had to *know* the child was breathing. Jenny was a good baby. She was fed at ten o'clock at night and slept until five the following morning. Catherine was wakeful. At first Paul was sympathetic. Yes, he understood, he said. You can't put all your eggs in one basket so we'll have another child. He had meant in a little while, not right away.

'I would have liked to have had my wife back again for a bit longer,' he had said.

Simon was born when Jenny was crawling. Catherine frequently carried a child on each hip.

'You poor thing!' people would say. 'However do you manage!'

Catherine thought she managed very well.

Paul did not think she managed well enough.

He was an orderly man. His success in life was based on his ability to expose carelessness and inefficiency and to replace them with structure and adherence to rules. He was well known for the number of failing businesses he had rescued and set on the right path.

Catherine did not enjoy being treated as a failing business and, unlike the businesses, argued back.

The house was losing its pristine stylishness — so what? There were children in it. She was not the svelte, stylish creature she had been — she had children now and accepted the loss of elegance. Why couldn't he?

A time when tolerance was being tested

and patience wearing thin had not been the ideal moment to conceive again.

And it is not as though you were born of great love or overpowering passion, she apologised to the small person busy trying to unscrew the bolt that held the table of his chair in place. It had been more of a routine exercise, like the necessary running of a car engine to make certain the parts would continue to function.

What was it Henry Green asked?

How important was it that my children should be Paul's?

I did not answer him then, nor would I now, but I know the answer.

⋆ ⋆ ⋆

Henry Green.

The thought of him made her remember the possums.

'Come on, my lad,' she said to Barnaby, scooping him up. 'Let's go and have a look at those traps.'

It was a mercy she had taken his cot into her room. The cage outside the children's bedroom window was shut and the round shape of a sleeping possum was tucked up in one corner. There was blood about.

'O-ooh!' she said. The creature must have

battered its head against the bars of the cage. Poor thing — she would not have wanted that.

There was a possum in the other cage. There was more blood. Where are you, Henry Green?

She hurried downstairs and had picked up the phone before she realised she did not have his address or telephone number. Andromeda's Mrs Tims had told him where he was needed and he had come. She needed him again, now — but how to find him?

She began to panic. The poor little things could not be left in the cages. What did she do? Open them so they could escape?

Would they wake if she poked at them through the bars? Would they be safe abroad in daylight?

There was nothing for it, she would have to make the dreadful journey up to the shack on the hillside. And she only had Paul's meticulously maintained and sleekly polished Mercedes in which to drive there. She gave an exasperated moan. She would have to leave the car on the road and make the climb to find Mrs Tims with Barnaby papoosed to her back.

He will like that, she realised, her spirits suddenly lifting, and come on, Catherine, the exercise will do you good, and it's not as if time means anything to us today. We can eat in the village if we must — buy some jars of baby food — make an adventure of it.

★ ★ ★

Too much of a bloody adventure, she thought, struggling, panting up the rutted path. Her thigh muscles felt as though they were screaming in outrage. Barnaby was a ton weight at her back. I am *sweating*, she noticed in distaste. She was not pleased when she heard footsteps rattling the stones on the path behind her and a young woman said a pleasant 'Excuse me' and swung past her, striding confidently and breathing easily. Catherine hated her. She made her feel like an old nag drooping in the traces.

How right Henry Green had been. The first thing she must do was recover her health and strength. It isn't as though I am *old*, she told herself, and there can't be much wrong with my basic structure — after all I climbed Snowdon five times that summer. She tried to think of an Australian equivalent to the grandeur of crag and peak and could not. The Blue Mountains had never seemed mountains to her and she had never had the time to go further afield. The Blue Mountains. She thought of Paul and the children now in the

129

little town where English flowers bloomed in the gardens. They were flowers she considered *flowers*. She had tried, and failed, to have them grow in her own garden. Lupins and delphinium seedlings keeled over, roses developed black spot, snapdragons rust and her granny's bonnets were milliner's rejects. Fifteen years in Australia, she thought, and still bottlebrush and gazanias are foreign to me. Funny to think they will mean home to my children.

She was concentrating so much on her thoughts she became careless about where she set her feet and stepped on a jagged stone.

She staggered and fell, holding out her arms to break the fall. She heard the snap of bone, crisp as the breaking of a water biscuit. Barnaby set up a howl, his face close to her ear. For a moment she lay there, unbelieving, winded, unable to move and then, in a panic, struggled to get to her feet. Her scream of pain was as loud as Barnaby's wailing. Her right arm! God in heaven, she surely could not have broken her right arm!

The young girl who had passed her came rushing back.

'Hang on, hang on,' she said. 'Don't try to move.' She unstrapped Barnaby, who kicked and plunged and fought her.

'Andromeda!' the girl called, trying to control the flailing limbs. 'Mrs Tims!'

Her face down on the gravel, Catherine heard the crashing arrival of Andromeda, and Mrs Tims' unmistakable voice saying God Almighty and felt herself being gently turned over.

'I'm the district nurse,' the girl said. 'I was on my way to see Mrs Tims. Lucky.'

It was, too; she had a mobile phone.

★   ★   ★

But the luck did not hold.

Catherine's teeth were chattering.

'Shock,' the girl said. 'I must get you to a hospital.'

The ambulance was out.

It was a jolting, painful stumble down the rutted path to where Catherine had left Paul's car.

'Oh, God,' the girl said when she saw the gleaming Mercedes. 'I'm only used to a Mazda automatic.'

'I'll tell you what to do,' Catherine managed to say.

Barnaby was howling. It made difficult communication even more difficult.

Gears scraped, unwanted wipers came on, the clutch leapt out.

'Hang on, hang on,' the girl said. 'If I can get it into second . . . '

Juddering, at a snail's pace, she eventually got the machine down the hill to the main road.

'Now!'

Hugging the curb and slow as a funeral procession they made their way towards the hospital.

'I'm going to be sick,' Catherine said.

'No, you're not. If I have to stop, I'll never get started again. And don't black out either. Shove her head down, Andromeda. O-ooh, up yours!' There was impatient tooting from the car behind. There was a lot of tooting from more than one car before she finally brought the vehicle to rest in front of the door of the emergency wing of the hospital. 'I can only deliver you,' she said. 'I'm sure somebody here will drive you home. God, am I glad I didn't prang this great brute.'

Her gratitude was nothing to that felt by Catherine. Paul would be impatient to find she had been stupid enough to break her arm; his anger if she had damaged his car was something she preferred not to think about.

★ ★ ★

132

It was late afternoon before they all got back home.

There had been a long wait at the hospital, first for X-rays and then for treatment. The nursing staff had been too busy and harassed to show much concern about anything so simple as a broken arm. The hungry Barnaby had become loudly fractious. Andromeda fed him on biscuits from the hospital kiosk and bottled fruit drinks, which made him burp.

Now he was hiccupy and fretful. He did not want to sit in his chair, he wanted to be cuddled and stretched out his arms in far from mute appeal.

With one arm strapped against her chest there was no way Catherine could pick him up. She sat on the floor by the side of his little chair and rubbed her head against his. She kissed his wet cheek and made crooning noises. That was not what he wanted at all. She bowed her head and they wept together.

Andromeda, busy in the kitchen, sang.

'I've put coriander in the omelette,' she said, a little while later, producing a tray, beautifully set with a tiny flower in a tiny cut-glass vase and a very large glass of gin and tonic.

Catherine reached for the gin. 'I don't feel like . . . '

'Yes, you do,' Andromeda said firmly.

'Don't drink all that now. Keep some for later.'

Out of politeness, Catherine ate. The omelette was lightly and crisply browned on the outside, smooth and delicate inside and deliciously tasty.

'Who taught you to cook like this?' she asked with respectful curiousity.

Andromeda laughed. 'Your books. You've got some brilliant ones. And I cut things out of magazines.'

'You've got a talent for it — a real flair. Did you know that?'

'I just like doing it.'

And that is the secret, Catherine noted to herself. When we like doing things we become good at them. Too bad all the things I like doing are no longer required of me.

The doorbell rang.

Andromeda went to answer it and came back followed by Henry Green.

'You!' Catherine cried.

'Yes,' he said, amused. 'Me.'

He looked her over with concern. 'Whatever happened to you?'

'It's all your fault,' she said, 'I was trying to find you.'

'But you surely knew I would come.'

'No, I didn't. You didn't say and you didn't leave me your address or phone number.'

'Because I knew I would be back today. Silly girl, you should have known too.'

She looked up into his face. The dark skin, the amused mouth, the scar across the eyebrow, the sag of skin beneath the chin, the kind eyes — all suddenly inexpressively dear. He was here. Everything would be all right now.

'Yes,' she said, 'I should have,' and felt the earth steady beneath her feet.

'Did you catch any possums?' Andromeda broke in.

'There are two in the traps,' she said, her treacherous voice breaking, 'and they have hurt themselves.'

'Hush,' Henry Green said, his hand warm on her good shoulder. 'I'll look after them.'

'Nosebleeds,' he informed her, after collecting the cages and taking them to his car. 'And they've probably given themselves nasty headaches, but nothing serious.'

She hoped he was not just saying comfortable words.

She wrung her hands. 'I only wanted them to stop frightening the children and making a mess of the mangoes.'

'And they have, but if you don't stop them getting into the roof you'll have to go through it all again.'

'How do I do that?'

'Plug the gaps under the eaves with chicken wire. Simple enough. Your husband could do it.'

'But he isn't here — he's away — and I don't know when he'll be back.'

She despised herself for the wail in her voice and pulled herself round. 'Tell you what. If I buy the chicken wire, would you fix it for me? Or don't rangers do things like that?'

He laughed. 'I've no idea. I'm not a ranger.'

'What do you do then?'

'I make up crossword puzzles.'

She stared at him with her jaw dropped.

'And do the chess column in the . . . '

'You're H.G.!' she burst out. 'My husband has trouble with you!'

'Crossword or chess?'

'Chess. I used to do the cryptic until . . . '

'You found better things to do.'

In so short an exchange of words a whole shift of relationship had taken place. Too much sock and a crumpled shirt collar became acceptable eccentricities and not — God, she thought, how can I still be so bloody English?

He was looking at her and smiling.

'I'll pick up the wire and come and do it tomorrow. How's that?'

'Fine.'

He got up to go. There was such a lot of him.

It's like having a liner moored alongside, she thought, smiling. I should wave him off with flags and bunting.

Andromeda had taken Barnaby's cot to her room in case he woke and Catherine was unable to lift him.

Catherine stood out on the balcony in the fading light and looked down on the open window of the girl's room. She could see Andromeda moving about and the shadow of the monstera leaves on the wall. Andromeda was dancing and singing, swinging Barnaby's small body in wide, graceful swoops far up and then down. His delighted uncontrollable laughter floated up to her. Steady, steady, she thought, tears before bedtime. But there were none. After a while Andromeda drew the curtains and put out the light and all was silent. Getting knickers off with one hand was not easy, and what the hell do I do about this bra? she wondered. Thought had not been given when her arm had been dealt with. And what do I do about having a shower?

A one-handed wash was all she could manage, and very unsatisfactory it was too. The unhooked bra escaped from the sling in which she had tucked it and dangled in the washbasin. She could not have it as her damp companion for the night. She found scissors. The cuts she was able to make using her left hand were far from neat. One good, expensive bra gone.

She was tired but could not sleep. To make sure Jenny and Simon were safe was always her crying need before she could settle down herself. But they were at Leura.

What do I do? Call Paul?

She lay and fretted, but doing anything was beyond her. Don't be silly, she told herself, they won't just die — Beth would call if anything were wrong.

To divert herself she thought of Henry Green sitting surrounded by dictionaries and reference books compiling his crossword puzzles. She tried to imagine what his house might be like and prowled around the imaginary rooms looking for photographs of his dead wife.

She did not hear the downstairs telephone ring.

⋆   ⋆   ⋆

'Come *on*!' Paul said impatiently drumming his fingers. 'It's only half past nine. She can't have gone to bed.'

Beth, standing at his shoulder, waiting to have a word with Catherine, shook her head.

'Perhaps she has,' she said gently. 'It's a good chance for her to have a rest.'

She laid her hand on his as he began to dial again. 'Leave it till morning, my dear. Your father wouldn't have wanted to spoil her night's sleep.'

'Just once more,' Paul demurred.

It was only an hour since he had watched his father die and he could not sit still and could not imagine how anyone could want a night's sleep.

'No,' Beth said firmly, taking the instrument from him and returning it to its rest. 'Not till morning.'

14

Catherine was wakened in the morning by an anxious Andromeda, saying urgently, 'Mr Grant! Mr Grant is on the phone.'

'Oh, God! What time is it?'

'Ten past nine.'

She moaned. What was the matter with her? Why was she sleeping so long? She had wanted to call Simon and Jenny.

This would be the *second* time he had caught her out. She knew what he would think.

Scrambling into her dressing-gown was awkward and took time; her strapped arm seemed to affect her balance and she had to go downstairs step by step. By the time she picked up the phone he was tight with temper.

'Do you know the time?' he accused her. 'You can't leave everything to Andromeda!'

'I'm sorry. I was . . . '

He didn't care how she was.

'I rang last night but could get no answer.'

'Did you?' she said bemusedly. 'I went to bed early.'

'I would have thought you could have

stayed up long enough to wait for my call. Or at least to have felt enough concern to ring here before you went to bed. Or remembered you do have a mobile telephone.'

She should have, of course. He was quite right, but the arm . . .

I'm sorry,' she said genuinely. 'How is he?'

'He's dead.'

He shot the words at her viciously as though to punish her.

He succeeded.

Guilt and grief swept over her, robbing her of speech.

Dear Ned. Such a nice man.

'At least he was able to see the children,' she managed at last.

'He was unconscious by the time we got here.'

He was determined to spare her nothing.

'The funeral will be early next week,' he said. 'We haven't arranged it yet. You had better be here by Tuesday. I need my car to take Beth . . . '

'Of course,' she interjected.

'Well, I'll let you go back to bed then,' he said, and rang off.

She was still sitting in a sodden heap when Henry Green arrived bearing chicken wire.

'She's had bad news!' Andromeda cried, planting herself in front of Catherine with her arms outstretched and making it clear that, in her book, ladies wearing intimate garments were not for the sight of casual callers, especially when the intimate garments were so inefficiently draped.

Henry Green had no such scruples. He brushed Andromeda aside and knelt down beside Catherine. 'My poor girl,' he said, and put his arm round her shoulders. With a great sob she turned, her head butting into his shoulder, her strapped arm awkward.

'There now,' he murmured, and moved her round gently so that she rested comfortably against his great chest and the pillow of his stomach. 'There now.'

He looked up questioningly at the open-mouthed Andromeda.

'Her father-in-law has died,' the girl explained, obviously thinking the grief excessive for the occasion. 'And she needs to get dressed.'

'So she does.' He smiled up at her conspiratorially. 'Tell you what. You see to that and I'll go and deal with this chicken wire. Come on now, help me get her up.'

'I can get myself up,' Catherine said, struggling. There were limits.

* * *

She was decently dressed and in what passed for her right mind when he came back down the ladder and pronounced the roof as possum-proof as he could make it but said he could offer no guarantees. 'They're cleverer than me,' he added.

Catherine gave him an old-fashioned look of gratitude.

You're clever enough, she thought. She had noticed how Andromeda's defensiveness had melted when exposed to little more than a dozen of his quiet words. She had made them coffee — a big pot — brought it into the sitting room and retired to the kitchen with Barnaby.

'Come and sit down,' Catherine said, 'and don't worry, I can pour with my left hand.'

There were bits of creeper in his hair and his hands were scratched and dirty. He held them up. 'Could I . . . ?'

'Of course.'

He could easily have washed them in the kitchen or the downstairs loo but she directed him upstairs, to her bathroom.

When he came down she was amused to see the creeper was still there.

He settled expansively in the large chair and leaned forward and picked up the small cup of coffee she had poured. It looked ridiculous in his hand.

She gave an exasperated laugh and got up abruptly. 'Sorry. Andromeda believes in gracious living. I'll get us some decent-sized breakfast cups.'

When she came back from the kitchen he was smiling.

'What?' she said.

His smile widened. 'You please me.'

He said it so openly she did not know how to respond.

'Yes . . . well . . . it's good coffee.'

'It certainly is.'

Was he laughing at her?

'I don't know how it is,' she began, taking charge, 'but every time we meet there seems to be a crisis of some sort.'

'I'm sorry about your father-in-law,' he said, picking up the nuance very quickly.

'He was only in his sixties.'

'Your mother-in-law?'

'She'll be devastated but she won't make a fuss.'

'Your husband?'

'Taking it badly. I don't think he realised how much it would mean . . . and he's very angry, particularly with me. You know how it is, you have to take it out on someone. And I've made a complete mess of things — again. I didn't tell him about my arm.'

'What?'

'I hardly got the chance. The state he was in! I shirked butting in and telling him. It would just have been another thing to hold against me. And now I don't know what the hell I am going to do. He is expecting me to drive his car up there, for the funeral — he took mine because of the seats for the children — and it's hardly funeral-standard, as you may remember.'

'Where is 'up there'?'

'Leura.'

'Well, that's not too far.'

'With one hand — and a lively baby!'

'I'd drive you.'

She could find nothing to say.

'You could tell him you'd hired this man from the village . . . '

'But . . . ' she stammered, 'but . . . how would you get back?'

'Ever heard of the train?'

She felt her throat thicken. 'I couldn't ask . . . '

'You don't have to. Barkis is willin'.'

Damn the man. He either made her laugh or cry. 'Oh, I don't know,' she said helplessly.

Andromeda appeared. 'He's had his lunch so we're going for a walk,' she said. 'Don't try and take those cups out to the sink. Leave them for me.'

When she had gone they sat and looked at each other.

'I hate to see you so unhappy,' he said. 'We can surely work something out.'

'Oh, I don't know . . . ' she said again.

'Well, I do.'

He got up and came and sat beside her on the couch and got up again.

'No, that's your bad side.'

He settled himself comfortably on her good side.

'Ring him now, tell him about your arm and say he's not to worry, you have a driver who can bring you and the car to Leura and that everything will be all right. Be calm about it; he'll have a lot on his plate so don't alarm him.'

'You wouldn't have to take the train,' she said, brightening. 'You could drive my car with the children — that would mean I'd have to come with you and Paul could drive himself back.'

'So,' he said, 'take a deep breath and make your call.'

Obediently she dialled the Leura number.

'Oh,' Paul said. 'It's you.'

She had to take another deep breath.

'Now don't get upset,' she said, 'everything's under control.'

'That means there's plenty to be upset

146

about,' he cut in. 'What now?'

'I've broken my arm.'

'God above!' he said in exasperation. 'How did you do a silly thing like that?'

'Never mind. I'm all bound up and have everything organised. A man from the village will drive me and Barnaby up for the funeral in your car and bring me and the children back in mine.'

She heard his horrified intake of breath.

'The Mercedes! Do you think I would let some oaf drive the Mercedes! You'll have to take the train. Damn and blast! I'll have to hire a car up here.'

'Paul,' she said, 'I have a broken arm. I couldn't carry Barnaby on the train.'

'No,' he conceded after a pause. 'I suppose not.'

'So what do we do?'

'God knows.'

She waited. She was regaining her control and her cynicism. She doubted if the Almighty would reveal much to Paul.

'Better stay where you are,' he said at last. 'You wouldn't be much use here. One good thing is Beth has asked if the children can stay on for a while — it will help to tide her over. I said I didn't know if you'd be agreeable, but now . . . Andromeda will have enough to contend with with you and Barnaby.'

'Good thinking,' she said carefully, thinking viciously to herself that it was good for everyone but her. Doesn't he know how much I will miss them? 'Now would you please let me speak to Beth?'

'She had a bad night. She's asleep.'

She didn't know whether to believe him.

'Then I'll have to rely on you to give her my love and tell her I am thinking of her.'

He made a noise that she presumed signified assent.

'One more thing,' she said. 'I will be sending my own flowers. My own. Do you understand? Don't include my name with yours on the ones you choose.'

When she put the receiver down she was shaking.

'Do I have to tell you or did you hear?' she asked Henry Green.

'I heard. I was driving expensive cars before he developed his first pimple.'

She was glad to find he had bite.

'Oh, God,' she said, 'what a dreadful two days.' Her nerves were vibrating like piano wires.

He laid his warm firm hand on her trembling shoulder.

'S-ssh.'

The hand began to stroke.

'There, there,' he said.

She drew a long, unsteady breath.

'Do you know what would do you good?' he asked.

'M-mm?' She had not been stroked so lovingly since she was a child.

'A lovely, long, long massage,' he said.

Behind her closed eyes she saw him as she had first seen him — a big, ungainly man who turned his feet out as he walked and showed too much sock. She had wondered amusedly and affectionately what he would look like in his underpants. She began to laugh.

'Do you think we'll be able to manage?' she said.

15

'Sit down! Read a book! I don't know why you didn't stay in bed,' Andromeda scolded.

Last night Catherine, determined not to backslide again, had set the alarm on her bedside radio and, this morning, had risen at an early and exemplary hour.

'You're always knackered and when you have the chance of a rest you don't take advantage of it.'

Catherine sighed. She not only could not please all of the people all of the time, but some people she did not seem able to please any of the time. She meanly pulled rank. 'That's enough,' she said sharply.

'But you *worry* me!'

Authority was no match for affection.

'I'm sorry,' she said contritely. 'I didn't mean to snap.'

'Oh that's all right,' Andromeda was airy. 'I know it's only your arm talking. People say funny things when they're in pain.'

Paul had certainly come out with some 'funny things'. And she knew he was in pain. How airy could *she* be about it?

'He must have been good-looking when he

was young, that possum chap,' Andromeda said with a complete volte-face that momentarily took Catherine's breath away.

'He's not bad looking now,' she said with forced joviality.

'He lives in that big house down by the beach. Mrs Tims used to go there when his wife was alive.'

'To do the cleaning?'

'No!' Andromeda's laugh was full-throated. 'Dulcie's no cleaner! She just went there to see them.'

Dulcie Tims paying a social call! The idea was ludicrous.

'People *like* her,' Andromeda added defensively, picking up on her expression. 'She's very kind. She's been unknown good to *me*. People are always coming up to visit her.'

The world must be full of masochists! 'Whoever would *choose* to make such a climb! Whatever do they come for?'

'I dunno. They just sit and talk.'

'Ah,' Catherine said, feeling that there could only be one possible explanation.

'I get it! She tells fortunes! Cross-my-palm-with-silver stuff!'

'No!' Andromeda was outraged. 'She'd kill you if she heard you say that! She'd never take money!'

'Then what is it all about?'

151

'I don't know! I asked her once and she told me it was nothing to do with me. And when I said go on, tell me, she went all jokey. 'I can smell the weather for folks,' she said.'

Catherine was not interested in Dulcie's jokes, she wanted to know about the puzzling connection between her and Henry and his wife.

Andromeda was getting tetchy.

'All I know is she thinks the world of him. He gave up his practice to look after his wife.'

'What was wrong with her?'

'Cancer,' Andromeda replied, as though it could hardly have been anything else.

'And what was his practice?'

'He was a vet.'

It was all falling into place. A vet. That explained his knowledge of possums and why he could show such wordless intuition.

She pictured him sitting by the bedside, playing chess by himself, and making up crossword puzzles. Her throat thickened as she thought of the way she had looked forward to her tussles with H.G.

'I think I will go and lie down,' she said.

She was overcome with the need for time and space in which to try to cope with all the new things that had come into her life.

Yesterday for example.

She had, of course, had massage before.

This one was different.

His hands were warm, strong, knowing.

'Oh, yes,' she said, '*there*!'

The movement was slow, rhythmic, assured, unerring in finding need.

'A-aah,' she breathed.

'That's the girl. Let go — let go.'

She drifted, totally aware, totally absorbed. The silence sang.

She felt it as surely as though they had both taken a physical step. A threshold had been crossed; now there was communication — deep, elemental. It is as though we are both listening to the same music, she thought.

It was better than making love.

Paul was a kind lover, never leaving her without climax, but a certain amount of tinkering was needed before they could reach their own destinations in their own time.

There would be no tinkering by Henry. He would *know*.

Her vagina clenched. She would have liked to have rolled over and drawn him down.

And he knew, she was sure. And he wanted it too. Desire cannot be hidden.

She remembered the friendly slap on the bottom and the 'Up you get!' but also the intensity he was not quite quick enough to hide behind the bland smile.

Dear Henry, she thought. Dear, dear Henry.

'Telephone,' said Andromeda, appearing at the bedroom door. 'Says she's Miss Gordon.'

'Janie!'

'Sorry about this,' Janie said, 'but I thought I ought to ask you. Beth has told me about Ned.'

It took a moment for the sense of it to sink in. Of course Janie was bound to know Paul's parents — he would have taken her to see them — after, all theirs had been a long-time relationship.

'Sad, isn't it?' she said. 'He was such a nice man. I suppose you were fond of him too.'

'Yes,' Janie said. 'Very. And of Beth.'

'Whatever will she do now?'

'I can't imagine.'

Janie cleared her throat. 'The thing is,' she said, 'what do I do about the funeral? Beth has asked me to go. She can't have been thinking straight.'

'What do you mean? She obviously wants people he cared about there. Of course you must go.'

'But what about you? What about Paul?'

'What about me? You surely don't think I'd . . . oh, come on, Janie! What sort of an idiot do you think I am?'

'It's not so much you. It's Paul.'

'Oh, *bugger* Paul!' Catherine burst out. 'If Beth has asked you, you must go. Anyway, I can't be there. I've broken my arm.'

'*What?*'

'I'm all trussed up and I can't drive.'

'You could go on the train.'

'That's what Paul said.' Catherine was becoming acid. 'What do I do about Barnaby? Carry him in my teeth?'

'You could leave him with that girl of yours for one day surely.'

She had not thought of that.

'I could too,' she said slowly.

She thought about it now.

'On the other hand,' Janie put forward tentatively, 'you could drive up with me.'

Now that was a thought which needed digesting.

There was a silence. Then 'No,' they cried simultaneously.

'I don't think we could do that to him,' Janie said.

'He's feeling bad enough,' Catherine agreed.

'I'm sure.'

They fell silent again.

'Why are we so *nice* to him?' Catherine asked.

'It's Beth I worry about.'

'Her sister is bound to be there . . . and

she's a nurse . . . '

'And Paul's brother — he's used to drama. Did you ever meet his friend?'

'The over or underwhelming one?'

'Don't tell me there are *two*!'

They were slipping into comfortable family gossip.

Janie brought them back to the problem.

'*You* should be there.'

'So should you. On the other hand, maybe neither of us should. We should leave Paul and his mother together — without intruders.'

'You're right,' Janie said with relief.

'But what I think we *should* do is to go up and see Beth together — when it's all over. Go for *her*.'

'Right again,' Janie said with a suspicion of tears in her voice. 'You're on.'

*   *   *

'It's nice to see you smile for a change,' Andromeda commented when Catherine joined her in the kitchen.

*   *   *

'No need for that look,' Janie told the black-browed Eve. 'She's not as bad as all that.'

16

'You are a hard man, Henry Green,' Catherine declared, doing as instructed and passing him another bottle of pills from her collection only to see it cast into the wastebin. 'That lot is only six months over the use-by date.'

'Knock it off,' he said. 'I am a *serious* man and this won't do.'

The dark-skinned face, which bore the scars of adolescent acne, was heavy.

She regarded it indulgently and affectionately; it was as though sight had acquired another dimension.

All that now remained from her pharmacopia sat lined up on the kitchen counter: a half-used bottle of yeast tablets, an unopened container of mega-vitamin C pills, and a plastic container on which was written EVENING PRIMROSE — DO NOT FORGET.

'Woeful,' he said.

She sat on her high stool, prim as a schoolgirl awaiting instruction, and alight with joy.

'Tell me,' she said, charming as all get-out.

He was not charmed. 'Knock it *off*,' he cautioned.

So this is what being pulled into line means, she thought amusedly, and felt her amusement die as he got up and began to walk towards the kitchen door.

'Henry!'

He turned.

She never wanted him to look at her so impassively again.

'Sorry,' she said. 'So sorry. Please don't go.'

He did not move. He stood and looked at her as though considering the options.

'I mean it,' she said.

'What do you mean?'

She stared at him helplessly. 'I don't know.'

'Well,' he said, confusing her further by again becoming the comfortable, easy person she had thought him, 'we'll have to find out, won't we?'

★ ★ ★

'If one has a problem,' Henry Green said, 'it is only sensible to identify it, isolate it, stand it up and walk round it, examining it from every side, and then decide if there is or is not anything to be done to get rid of it. If there is, and there nearly always is, one sets about it. If there is more than one problem, and there

158

nearly always is, they are taken one at a time.'

'What you are telling me,' said Catherine, 'is that I have made a right cat's breakfast of my problems.'

'I am?' The humour was back in his face.

'Oh, come on, Henry, you know you are. And I have. And what the hell *is* a cat's breakfast?'

The kitchen was warm with sunlight; breakfast things tidied away, sink and draining-board gleaming, the coffee pot, tin of coffee and filters standing waiting beside the equally gleaming kettle. Andromeda had been at work. Now she was away cleaning the bathrooms and Barnaby was sitting in his play-chair picking the stuffing out of a toy rabbit.

'That child is a destroyer,' she said. 'He takes everything to pieces. And Andromeda is not required to clean but I can't stop her. There are two problems for you.'

'Catherine,' he said, 'am I going to have trouble with you?'

'Oh, all right,' she said, giving in, 'I've been stupid. I knew what I should have done — but I never got round to doing it properly. I bought all the right remedies but there was so much else to think of I kept forgetting to take them. I was sloppy. So now I'm tired all the time, bad-tempered most of it and can't fit into my clothes. That do you?'

'To start with.'

'That sounds as though we are in for a long haul.'

'We are, aren't we?'

And what was behind the steadfast eyes as he said *that*?

She looked right back at him. 'Oh, yes,' she said, 'certainly. We are.'

And whatever my troth is, Henry Green, she thought, I have plighted it.

'Then,' he said, 'we will take first things first.'

First things were the purchases of vitamin E capsules, garlic capsules and complex vitamin B tablets. 'You have enough vitamin C,' he conceded.

'Zinc would probably be good for you too and you need iron. I will tell you what sort to get. We don't want you constipated.'

Reference to her bowels was disconcerting and she was further taken aback when he added, 'And we've got to do something about that bladder.'

Now that it was mentioned it made itself evident. She crossed her legs neatly and sat up straight. Goddamn it, she had only recently been.

'Not to mention your nerves.'

'I bet your animals were glad you didn't

160

talk to them!' she burst out.

'How did you know I was a vet?'

'I have my spies.'

He would know the information could only have come through Dulcie Tims.

'Not that she's a friend of mine,' she said hastily.

'Well, she is of mine.'

He was looking peaceful and amused.

'I was very sorry to hear about your wife. Very sorry.'

'It was a bad time.'

It was obviously all he was going to say.

'Do you want to make a list and get Andromeda to go to the health food shop for you? Or would you like me to drive you down to the village to get everything?'

She weighed up the choices.

Barnaby was due for sleep — they would be virtually alone in the house. The thought was tempting.

But there was something beguiling about the idea of their going out together on a joint enterprise.

'We'll go,' she decided, and took pleasure in using the personal pronoun.

'Mr Green has returned one of the possum traps in case we need it again,' Catherine told Andromeda, 'and since I can't drive he has very kindly offered to take me down to the

161

village to do some shopping.'

'Have you got a list?' Andromeda asked quickly. 'We're clean out of black pepper and cornflour, and how about some of that blue stuff for the loos?'

'Perhaps you would like me to get some nice little covers for the seats too?' Catherine asked acidly.

'Now that's an idea!'

'This girl is *thick*,' Catherine muttered to Henry.

'No. Just unaccustomed to sarcasm,' he replied coldly.

Oh, dear, this *was* a day for the slapping of the wrist.

'Pay attention,' he said. 'Lists must be made.'

'The biochemic tissue salts, ferrum phosphate and potassium phosphate. As well as all the other things.'

'Tissue salts!' said Andromeda in delighted recognition. 'You gave Mrs Tims them, didn't you? — when her liver was playing up.'

'Different ones.'

'She swears by them. 'Where's me pills?' she says, soon as she sees the spots.'

'Mrs Tims suffers from migraine,' Henry told Catherine.

She didn't much care what she suffered from and was annoyed to find that she, Catherine, was not alone in his concern.

162

'Shall we go?' she asked. 'And I trust your car does not reek of possum.'

'Alas it does. But we'll keep the windows open.'

Did he always have to look so amused?

The purchases were made.

Back at home the medicaments were lined up and dosages and times decided.

'Write it all down,' Henry Green insisted. 'Three times. On three separate cards. Attach one to the fridge, another to your wardrobe door and prop one against your bedside light.'

'Oh, come on!'

'You mean I can trust you?'

'I'll see she takes them,' Andromeda chipped in.

No, you bloody won't, Catherine said to herself, this is between Henry and me.

'You will have to write the cards,' she told him triumphantly.

He wrote them.

'The next thing is tension,' he said. 'Sit down, Andromeda, this will help you too.'

'Oh, goody,' Andromeda said brightly, and sat.

Catherine would have preferred her to have showed a proper reticence and taken herself off. Surely there were taps she was longing to polish.

'It is ridiculously simple,' he said, 'but most good things are.'

'Are you sitting comfortably?'

Catherine suppressed a sudden urge to laugh. As though we are kids about to listen to a fairytale, she thought.

'Mrs Grant!'

She bowed her head contritely.

'Take a deep, deep breath,' he began, 'now let it come out slowly as you count three, three, three. Slowly. Take another deep breath — let it out slowly counting two, two, two. No hurry, no hurry at all. Now take another deep breath. Let that one go, counting slowly one, one, one. Stay quiet. Breathe slowly and gently. Stay where you are.'

The calm, quiet voice became silent.

Catherine stayed where she was — wherever it was — grateful to be there. The world had slowed down; she was cushioned and eased; her brittleness softened like toffee left in sunlight.

'You see!' Henry Green said mischievously as she opened her eyes.

'Wow!' said Andromeda, stretching and yawning.

Softened Catherine might feel, prepared to share any further she was not.

'How about seeing if Barnaby is awake yet?' she said.

With a backward, reluctant look, Andromeda headed for the door.

'Look out!' Catherine cried, but too late. Andromeda had already stumbled over Barnaby's rabbit, left lying on the floor, and had come down heavily, hitting her head against the door as she fell.

'I don't believe this!'

That two able-bodied women should do themselves damage within so short a space of time was ridiculous.

'O-oo-ooh!' Andromeda moaned and clasped her head as Henry Green bent over her.

At least she had the use of her arms. 'Can you get up?' Catherine asked anxiously. All we need is a broken leg, she thought.

Both Andromeda's legs were sound, though she swayed alarmingly as Henry Green drew her to her feet.

'Hold on to her,' he instructed Catherine, and took a little bottle from his pocket.

'What's that?'

'Rescue Remedy.'

Oh, well, if he wanted to be funny . . .

She watched as he persuaded Andromeda to open her mouth a little so that he could squirt some of the liquid under her tongue. Then he squirted some more onto his fingers and rubbed them gently on the part of her temple that had hit the door. 'Come on now, sweetie,' he said, 'let's sit you down.'

He put his arm around her shoulders and steered her through to the sitting room, where he installed her on the couch, putting her feet up and adjusting cushions.

The sight of Andromeda's chalk-white face momentarily overcame the pang Catherine felt as she yet again became aware of his concern for another.

'Give her a minute or two and she'll be all right,' Henry said, 'and I don't suppose you happen to have any arnica ointment?' He did not sound very hopeful.

'As a matter of fact I have,' Catherine replied and went, with great dignity, to find it for him.

Actually she did not have it, Paul did. He used it for bruises he sustained while playing squash. Thank God it was there in his bathroom cabinet.

She produced it with the aplomb of a conjurer producing a rabbit out of a hat.

He gently applied some to the lump, which was rising like dough on Andromeda's forehead. 'That will do it,' he said comfortingly.

They sat and watched Andromeda with the attention given to a movie screen. Colour gradually returned to her cheeks.

'Is that thing going down?' Catherine asked in disbelief.

'It will,' he said.

When Barnaby's piercing shrieks reached them there was nothing else for it. 'I'll get him,' Henry said.

'Talk about the halt and the lame,' Catherine quipped, just as she had the day they first met at the beach. Andromeda laughed shakily, 'at least we're not blind.'

I don't know about that, Catherine thought. The way ahead had never seemed less clear.

It was hard to believe it was only just lunchtime.

'What does he eat?' Henry asked.

'Give him mashed banana and some cornflakes; he always eats them up,' Andromeda said quickly.

Catherine had been about to suggest part of a lightly boiled egg and a rusk. He did not always eat that up.

She pressed Andromeda back among the cushions. 'I have one hand. I can feed him.'

'Afterwards,' Henry said, 'if Andromeda feels well enough, I know a nice little café near the beach — it might be pleasant for us all to have lunch there.'

Paul would not approve of his wife being seen eating in a public place with the girl hired to look after the children — or the man paid to remove his possums. Paul was upwardly mobile. He knew how important it was to be seen with the right people.

'What a lovely idea,' Catherine replied. 'Some sea air will be good for all of us.'

Lunch was Greek salad and small, crispy fish and sticky toffee pudding. Barnaby became as sticky as the pudding.

'What a lovely time we're having,' Andromeda said.

Catherine felt the sun on her back, saw the table striped with shadow, the hands that dealt deftly with knife, fork, spoon, that reached out and touched hers to encourage her to eat and she couldn't remember when she had last felt so relaxed and happy.

'See where the sea meets the sky?' Henry Green said, looking out past the umbrellas and the coloured caps of bathers in the shallows. 'They say a fine green line appears just before the sun lifts over that horizon every morning.'

'Have you seen it?'

'Not yet.'

She smiled at him. It was the smile she kept for the intimate, seductive occasion. It was meant to say, 'Someday we will see it together.'

'Dulcie Tims told me about it,' he added, smiling back.

★   ★   ★

When they returned to the house the telephone was ringing.

'Catherine! What is this nonsense about you not going to Pa's funeral?' an irate voice said.

'Peter! Where are you?'

Paul's brother was never in one place for long.

'I'm in the city. Ma says you've broken your arm.'

'I have, and . . . '

'Well, that's no problem. I'll pick you up and deliver you back. I can only stay for the one day, so that . . . '

'But the baby?'

'Janie says you've got someone there to help. Surely she could manage for one day?'

'You've already spoken to Janie?'

'You weren't in. I got the same sort of nonsense from her. I told her bollocks, she was going. I'm picking her up then I'll collect you. Beth wants you both there, so bollocks to Paul too. I gather you were both being delicate about his feelings. Well, it's Ma's feelings that matter.'

169

'Rather a lot of 'bollocks' there, darling,' she rejoined.

'Well then,' he said, 'no argument.'

'Hang on.'

She turned to Andromeda. 'Could you manage Barnaby all day on Tuesday? Do you feel up to it?'

Andromeda fingered her bump. 'I suppose so,' she said and turned eyes that were as clear blue as the dress she was wearing on Henry Green.

'I'll come and take you for a drive if you like,' he said obligingly, 'and there are a lot of other nice places for lunch — that would take up most of the day.' He turned to Catherine. 'Would that make it easier for you?'

No, it wouldn't, she thought, and I'm damned if I'm giving Andromeda anything else to wear, but 'Yes,' she said. 'Thank you for being so helpful.'

If Andromeda's smile grew any wider her cheeks would be unable to stand the strain.

'The only thing is,' Catherine said, reclaiming Henry, 'funerals demand a hat. Would you take me back to the village to choose one?'

'Of course, but I think Andromeda should come too. She'll be more help than I could be.'

'Of course,' said Catherine, longing to lay into her.

★　★　★

Henry was left in the car with a newspaper and Barnaby.

'I didn't know there was a hat shop in the village,' Andromeda said.

'There isn't,' Catherine replied, making a determined beeline for the op-shop.

'You can't!' Andromeda was aghast.

'Oh, yes I can,' Catherine said. And did.

'That's what I want,' she told the lady manning the shop. 'That hat on the wig-stand.'

It was black felt, high-domed and wide-brimmed.

'I'll tart that up with a scarf and wear it with my black cape and red boots. It will be a knock-out. Come on.'

With the hat in a crumpled plastic bag they were back with Henry and Barnaby within minutes.

'That's what I call decisive shopping,' he said in admiration.

'You didn't think I could be decisive, did you?' she retorted, engaging his eye.

'Didn't I?'

She liked the way his mouth curved before

it broke into a smile. Oh, Henry Green! Henry Green! She enjoyed saying his name over and over in her mind like a litany. She enjoyed everything about him. She sank into the enjoyment as gratefully as she had sunk into the great pillowing comfort of his arms.

★ ★ ★

Paul telephoned.

'Peter tells me he has suggested picking up you and Janie Gordon and bringing you up here,' he said in a hard voice.

'Yes.'

'Don't even think of it!'

Catherine did not react well to peremptory orders.

'But I have thought.'

'I don't want her here.'

'But Beth does.'

'I'm sorry about that, but I still can't have it.'

One nice thing about Paul was the affection and deference he showed to his mother; that he could so blatantly disregard her wishes showed how deeply the humiliation heaped on him by Janie had affected him.

'Tell Peter not to pick her up then,' Catherine said.

'I can't. He didn't leave his telephone number. You must tell him.'

'I can't. I don't have it either.'

'Then you must tell Janie.'

'No. You tell her. You have her number.'

There was a black silence.

'I knew I could rely on you to make things worse,' he said at last. 'There's so much to do and I was up half the night with Simon. He has an earache.'

She immediately thought of meningitis and panicked.

'Then I must certainly come! I should have rung each day! I should have!'

'For God's sake,' he said wearily. 'Beth was a nurse. It's only a back tooth.'

'All the same, I'm coming.'

★   ★   ★

In the event neither she nor Janie went.

When Peter and Janie arrived early to collect her for the funeral she was holding Andromeda's head over a bucket in the bathroom. The girl was being violently sick and Barnaby, left alone in his cot, was shaking the bars and screaming like a train whistle.

Catherine shooed Peter on his way.

'You'll be late! Tell Beth I'll ring her

173

tonight. Tell her how we're fixed here, why we couldn't come.'

He left with alacrity.

'Which are you best at?' she asked Janie. 'Babies or people being sick? Oh, God, Andromeda! Not the other end too!'

'Babies,' Janie said firmly, put her bag down and took off in the direction of the piercing screams.

'I'm sorry. I'm sorry,' Andromeda moaned, her insides quite beyond control.

'Sit on the loo,' Catherine commanded. 'Hold the bucket on your lap.'

At least being a mother knocks the squeamishness out of you, she thought, tearing off lavatory paper and laying it over the brown liquid on the bathroom floor. If only I had two hands! She was in danger of bursting into hysterical laughter.

Andromeda was a sickly colour and damp to the touch. When she looked up at Catherine her eyes blazed a terrified blue.

'Have I been poisoned?' she croaked.

'Of course you bloody haven't!' Catherine said savagely, wondering if indeed Andromeda had and the same fate was about to overtake her. What were those crispy little fish they had eaten yesterday?

Janie appeared with Barnaby under her arm.

'What do I do with him?' she said.

Andromeda made a noise no words could describe and vomited violently into the bucket yet again. She took deep, ragged breaths and sank back against the lavatory cistern. Her eyes were closed, her lips slack.

'Oh, God,' Catherine said, 'what do we do?'

As they watched, the girl's breathing began to ease and her eyes opened. 'I think that's it,' she managed in a weak voice.

And indeed it was. She came back to herself with a speed it was hard to believe. The capacity of the young human body to recover was demonstrated to a grateful audience.

'I'm sorry,' she said yet again. 'I'm so sorry. Oh, look at the mess!'

'Never mind that,' Catherine said. 'Let's clean you up and get you out of here.'

'No! Don't touch me! Look after Barnaby. Please! Just leave me. I'll be all right. Go!'

Catherine, recognising Andromeda's need to keep face, took herself away.

It was only half past seven in the morning.

'Whatever time did you get up?' Catherine asked Janie.

'Dawn,' Janie said, 'and it feels like the end of the day already. That brother-in-law of yours is the definitive prophet of doom. I never want to hear another word about global warming and how desperate is the need to stop the population of the world increasing. I was dreading the drive up to Leura. He's so like Paul I thought even you might not have the courage to tell him to belt up.'

'He's worse than Paul. Paul does let you get a word in edgeways.'

'But he doesn't listen to it.'

They began to laugh.

Barnaby squirmed and Janie had to clasp him tightly.

'If you're going to help me with him I can't let you wear that suit. Babies are squalid little beasts.'

Janie's suit was dark grey and expensively cut. The white shirt-cuffs showing at the wrists were held together by gold cufflinks, the hands protruding from them were smooth and pale, the long fingers with their heavy rings had delicately coloured, beautifully shaped nails.

Just how I used to look, Catherine thought wryly.

'Lucky we're about the same size. I'll find something more suitable . . . '

'Not those cotton trousers!'

'No,' said Catherine smiling, 'I think I can do better than that. Keep him on your hip and we'll go up and see what we can find.'

'I shouldn't be here,' Janie said, keeping her eyes down and not looking around as they skirted the cardboard boxes and mounted the staircase.

'Well, you can hardly walk out on a sick girl, a one-armed woman and a helpless baby, can you?'

She must feel odd, Catherine reflected. She could have been the one living here with Paul. How does the house seem to her, I wonder? Does she think, with regret, this could have been mine, or does she look at me and think, with grateful relief, this could have been me? No prize for guessing which.

'What are you grinning at?' Janie asked, puffing. 'This child is wet. And I mean wet. I hope you're not expecting me to cope with it.'

'Not in that suit anyway,' Catherine teased, leading the way into the wardrobed connubial bedroom. 'Put him on the bed.'

'But he's wet!'

'So?'

Wetness when one had children was a way of life. Their wetness and your own. Janie planted him in the middle of the bed and sniffed at her jacket.

'You don't notice it till later,' said Catherine, 'usually in a crowded room.'

★　★　★

Clothes Catherine could no longer wear fitted Janie beautifully. The zip slid upwards easily and the material did not strain over the thighs; shirt buttons lay flat with no bulge between the buttonholes.

'God, you look good,' Catherine breathed in open envy.

But the face between the honey colour of the hair and the honey colour of the shirt was indoor pale and the heels of the shoes were far too high.

Janie needed open air.

'Thongs,' Catherine said. 'Must find you some thongs.'

'Sandshoes,' Janie corrected quickly, 'if you have any.'

She had. And they fitted.

'There you are then,' Catherine said with satisfaction.

'Now what about you?'

'Oh, God,' Catherine said, calling on the Creator yet again as she realised she was still in the dressing-gown that bore evidence of Andromeda's catastrophe and that Henry Green would be arriving and that getting into clothes when one arm is in a sling takes time and that without a bra the bosom sags — and how the hell could she fasten one?

'I'm here,' Andromeda sang out, material-ising in the doorway just in time to scoop up Barnaby, who was in danger of rolling off the bed. She was looking very pink and scrubbed and smelled strongly of disinfectant.

'O-ooh,' she said to Janie, 'don't you look great!'

Why do people who wear my clothes look so much better in them than I do? Catherine wondered crossly, remembering Henry Green's appreciation of the way the blue dress she had given to Andromeda had dramatised the hitherto unnoticed blue of her eyes. And what will he think when he sees this calm and lovely creature?

'Are you feeling up to feeding him?' she said to Andromeda.

'And how about making some coffee?' she suggested to Janie, hustling her towards the door. 'Andromeda will show you where everything is.'

She urgently needed to deal with her own appearance, which needed so much dealing with.

★ ★ ★

When she came downstairs, bra-less, the soft folds of the long Indian cotton dress she had managed to struggle into floating behind her and her eyes slanting green under lavender lids, Janie looked at her quizzically.

'So this is how you dress to look after babies, is it?' she asked wickedly. 'Who's coming?'

'Just somebody to pick up Andromeda,' she responded lightly. 'And what do you think of the house?'

'Wonderful.'

'I want Paul to sell it.'

'Good heavens, why?'

'It doesn't do.'

'What do you mean?'

'Take a look.'

'I am. It's . . . It's . . . '

Elegant, dramatic, expensive, guaranteed to provoke envy. Catherine supplied the words for her in her mind.

'You can see Paul written all over it, can't you?' she said aloud.

'Without doubt.'

'I'm waiting for the kids to break their necks falling down the stairs, tipping over the balconies or drowning in that bloody great pool. This house is for the people we were before we had them. I've changed. Paul hasn't.'

'And what do you want now?'

Catherine did not have to think. She recited her litany.

'And what does Paul say?'

180

'Do I have to tell you?'

She did not. Janie was the one person for whom explanation and interpretation were unnecessary.

'I'm glad you're here,' Catherine exclaimed impulsively.

'Yes . . . well . . . '

They looked at each other wordlessly, each aware of past history and future possibilities — but for Paul they would have been friends. There was no need to spell it out.

Janie touched her briefly on the shoulder. 'I think it's time we rang Beth,' she said.

'Oh, God, yes. You make me ashamed. I'd almost forgotten. And Simon has earache.'

Janie dialled the number and put the call on speaker so they both could hear.

Peter answered. He must have driven like the clappers.

'She's holding up well,' he said, 'you know Beth. She's sorry you can't be here but she understands. I forgot to ask — do you want me to pick you up on my way home?'

'Yes,' Janie said.

'No,' said Catherine.

Her mind was running ahead. If Janie stayed overnight Catherine could ask Henry Green to drive her to the city in the morning.

She took the phone from Janie and flicked it off speaker. 'Let me speak to Beth.'

'She's with the doctor.'

'I thought you said . . . '

'Not for her. For Simon.'

Panic hit. Her stomach muscles cramped.

'Let me speak to the doctor! Don't argue! Go and get him!'

He clicked his tongue and sighed. 'Bossy as ever,' he said. 'Hang on.'

'His temperature is high,' the doctor explained, 'and he's fretful. But you know what children are like. He could be as right as rain by evening. No, no,' he said, silencing her, 'it's not mastoid, it's not meningitis and I doubt if it's a brain tumour. Come on, Mum, you've seen it all before, I'm sure.'

'But I've always been *there*.'

'I think you can trust your mother-in-law.'

'But she has the funeral. She can't be at home with him!'

'I'll let you speak to her,' he said, withdrawing gratefully.

'You poor dear,' said Beth, 'what a time you are having.'

Catherine burst into tears and gave the phone to Janie. Everybody is so much nicer than I am, she thought. I only think of me but in spite of all her grief Beth thinks about other people.

Janie talked quietly to Beth, keeping a weather eye on Catherine.

'OK?' she asked when Catherine had regained her composure, and handed the instrument back to her.

'Sorry, Beth,' Catherine said. 'I'm all over the place. I'm worried about how you are managing.'

'Paul has been very helpful — he is very good with practicalities — and people have rallied round. I didn't know I had so many friends. Don't worry about Simon. I only called the doctor to make absolutely sure.'

'But how will you cope with him and the funeral?'

'A friend will stay at home with him and Jenny . . . '

'Will they . . . ?'

'They like her. They'll be fine. She will bring her own grandchild. Now stop worrying.'

'Oh, Beth, I ought to be helping you . . . '

'You didn't choose to break your arm or for your girl to fall ill.'

I bet Paul thinks I did, she thought.

'I love you, Beth,' she said.

'I know.'

The quiet assurance was like a blessing.

'Are you sure you want the children to stay afterwards?'

'I would be grateful.'

'When will Paul be coming home?'

'Tonight, I imagine. He can get a lift with Peter.'

'But don't you want one of them to stay on with you?'

'No.' The answer was crisp and definite. 'Give my love to Janie. I'd love to see her. Perhaps she would drive up with you when you're fit enough to cope with the children again. Is that arm painful?'

'Oh, Beth!'

Janie took over the phone again. When she put it down she turned to Catherine.

'Do you know what she called us? 'My two girls'.'

Catherine was awash once more.

'You certainly shouldn't wear eye make-up,' Janie joked and surprised them both by giving Catherine a sudden hug.

17

By the time Henry Green was due to arrive to collect Andromeda, Janie was feeling fraught.

'Your child weighs a ton,' she declared, planting Barnaby on the kitchen counter and applying her fists to the small of her back in a gesture Catherine knew only too well. Andromeda leapt forwards with a squawk and prevented him from poking his fingers into the electrical socket.

'Let me have him,' she said, implying that it was unsafe to leave him to anyone else.

'You broke your arm on purpose,' Janie said. 'I can see that now. Self-defence.'

Catherine was accustomed to having children attached to her like leeches and hanging from her like weighty ornaments.

'You could be right,' she smiled. 'The subconscious can be crafty.'

Their laughter roused Andromeda's displeasure. 'I'm not ready yet,' she said severely.

The reminder of Henry Green's impending arrival sent Catherine's hand flying to her hair. 'Can you help me with this?' she said to Janie anxiously.

'My word, you must be expecting someone important.'

'The possum man,' Catherine said treacherously.

'A friend. He's taking me and Barnaby for a drive and out to lunch,' Andromeda said proudly.

'That was when we thought I wouldn't be here,' Catherine pointed out. 'Things have changed now.'

Andromeda looked stricken.

'Now, now.' Catherine said, 'No need to go all tragic on me. We can probably make some other arrangements.'

'I have to make arrangements about getting home. I can't be here when . . . ' Janie's eyebrows were lifted significantly.

You certainly can't, Catherine silently agreed, cats would be among pigeons, fur would certainly fly.

'Do you know anything about the buses?' she was being asked.

'Nothing,' she said grandly. 'You don't imagine I would let you go home by public transport?'

'Perhaps Mr Green would . . . ' Andromeda began.

'Of course!' Catherine cried, as though she had never entertained such a thought. 'What a brilliant idea! We will ask him. We could go for a drive, have lunch and then take Janie home. It would make an outing for all of us!'

'Great!' Andromeda said, and shot off to get ready.

'My hair only needs looping up and pinning at the back,' Catherine said, 'but it's hard to do with just one hand.'

'Getting changed, having hair done — I'm intrigued. What's with this Mr Green?' Janie asked, smiling.

'You'll see. You'll see when you've met him,' said Catherine, unwilling to give anything away.

* * *

When he arrived he was wearing grey flannels, a blue shirt and a tweed jacket of mixed blue, green and heather colour. It looked as prickly as gorse.

My own stretch of moorland, Catherine thought, her lips twitching.

He looked larger than ever.

'I gather you recognise my English tweed,' he said, 'but I wasn't expecting to see you.'

Her pleased thought that he must have put the jacket on out of deference to her was blown out of the water and she was further irritated when he added, 'I thought it would be too tough for the moths, but it isn't. This is its last outing.'

'Don't you want to know why I'm here?' she asked tartly, leading him into the sitting room and telling him why in graphic detail.

'I thought she was going to die. It must have been those little fish you gave us for lunch.'

'Well, you ate them, and look at you.'

His tone implied that she looked not only healthy but lovely. That was better. 'Come and meet my friend,' she said, allowing herself to be mollified.

She made the introductions.

Janie offered her hand, which he took but did not shake, just pressed it warmly with his other hand and returned it to her.

'We have a problem,' Catherine told him, 'and Andromeda has thought of the solution. You are taking her out to lunch but since we are here, could we all come and afterwards could you be very, very kind and drive Janie home — to the city?'

'Why not?' he said amiably. 'There's just one thing though. I will be out longer than I expected so I must call at home and put out food for the cat. If I don't, I'll be in trouble. You know how offended cats can get.'

★ ★ ★

188

His station wagon did not have child seats. It was unsafe for babies to be nursed on the front seat, he said, and installed Barnaby with Andromeda on one side of him and Catherine on the other in the rear seat, with the safety harness cunningly adapted to contain them all.

Janie sat beside Henry at the front.

This was not what I had in mind, Catherine thought irritably. She could not hear what they were saying to each other. Andromeda was not looking pleased either. Catherine felt sorry for her. It had, after all, been her day out.

'Feeling better?' she asked, and gave the girl a warm smile over the top of Barnaby's head and received a watery one in return.

The damn man, Catherine thought, remembering how radiant the girl had been when she had thought it 'her' day — it's as though he creates the weather for us.

She herself was now feeling the heat of excitement. She was going to see where he lived. She badly needed to know where he was when he was not with her; she wanted evidence of what he *did*; she needed to see the bed in which he slept, the bathroom mirror into which he gazed, the brand of toothpaste he used. She was greedy for intimate knowledge.

He drove smoothly down to the village then swung off onto the winding road which led to the sea. The houses here were crouched low behind bushes and trees that gave them shelter. He turned into a cul-de-sac and pulled up in front of a gate in a tall brushwood fence. The house could not be seen.

She began to ease the constraining straps so as to be ready when he invited her in. He was not inviting her at all. He got out of the car, said, 'won't be a minute,' opened the gate and disappeared behind it, leaving her with the merest glimpse of lawn, bushes and the glint of glass.

'It's a really big house,' Andromeda told them. 'Mrs Tims says you need a bicycle to get round it. He's got his rooms and she had hers.'

Catherine had to bite back the urgent questions. Go on, she willed Andromeda, go on.

'You mean they lived separately?' Janie asked obligingly.

'Oh, no — they were all lovey-dovey. It was only for working. He had his vet clinic and she did her thing.'

Catherine swallowed. 'And what was that?'

'She made quilts.'

The long hours spent making small stitches

while your life was being eaten away, Catherine thought, and closed her mind at once. Pity for the dead was a waste of time. Now he was back and carrying a very large, very black cat.

'I've brought Tom to meet you,' he said. 'He likes to know what's going on.'

The cat regarded them all with yellow, indolent eyes.

'O-ooh,' said Janie, who was a cat person.

Catherine, who was not, remained silent.

Someone else to share him with, she thought irritably.

The animal allowed Janie to make much of him and made sinuous archings of the back and circlings of the shoulders. He had a purr like a lawn mower.

'He likes *you*,' Henry Green said warmly.

He brought the cat round to Catherine's window and found her consulting her watch. 'Are we in a hurry?' he asked.

'No-oo. Of course not.'

'Then have a word with the boy.'

'Has he any favourite topics of conversation?'

The smart, tart words were out before she could stop them.

Without answering he straightened up and turned away.

'I'll just get him settled,' he said, going

through the gate and closing it quickly behind him.

'I think he's cross,' Andromeda said.

Catherine knew he was.

I blew that one, she thought. Being clever gets me nowhere with him. And all right, if it's a case of love-me-love-my-cat, I'll love the bloody thing!

When he came back to the car and settled in she leant forwards and touched his shoulder.

'Sorry about that,' she said. 'It's just that I'm not feeling too good. My arm is painful.'

'Then we must do nothing that might hurt it,' he answered, and she was left to worry what he could mean by that.

★ ★ ★

Fortunately the day improved as it went on. Displeasure was no proof against the benevolence of the honeyed warmth of the sun and the soft wind. When they stood outside the little restaurant on the cliffs above the sea, they all breathed deeply and looked at each other with celebratory joy.

'You need a highchair for the child,' the waitress said.

'This is on me,' Janie stated.

Henry Green did not go all macho as Paul

would have done. 'That's very pleasant of you,' he said.

Andromeda hunched over her plate in a garlicky steam of happiness. 'Don't you just love prawns?' she cooed.

They were all saying the right things. Catherine was careful she should too. I am a quick learner, she congratulated herself.

When the meal was over they all went down to the beach. Janie and Andromeda took Barnaby out to the water to paddle and Henry made a comfortable nest among the rocks for himself and Catherine. She watched him at work and was alight with happiness.

She remembered how a beautiful woman she knew had explained her marriage to what had seemed a highly unlikely man. 'He has such good *hands*,' she had said, and Catherine had known what she meant. It was not just the warm, comfortable, willing and encompassing hand which took one's own, but the feeling of being *held*. The feeling one gets as he looks at me as he is looking now, his smile slow and indulgent.

'I feel so safe with you,' she said.

'Then you are on very dangerous ground. Learn to grow up, Catherine. Safety is not found in other people. Only in oneself.'

'Henry's homily?' she asked wickedly.

'You bet,' he said.

He settled himself comfortably beside her and looked out to where the others were splashing in the sea.

'Your friend is delightful.'

'My husband thought so too.'

'And then what happened?'

'Me,' she said.

He let it lie. He asked no more questions.

But she had a question of her own. She lifted his hand and pressed her warm, open lips into his palm. 'When are we going to make love?' she asked.

Before he could answer the other two women, flushed and laughing, came running towards them, swinging Barnaby between them. Catherine had never seen Janie so lovely. The careful elegance was gone; she looked artless, young and joyful.

She cast herself down beside Catherine.

'I've just realised,' she said, 'I'm still wearing your clothes. I've left mine . . . '

'There's no time to go back for them now,' Catherine cut in quickly. 'I presume you have another suit. Another pair of shoes?'

Her mind was working quickly. Here was an excuse to ask Henry to drive her into the city to return them.

She found, to her chagrin, that he was saying, 'I am seeing a chap in Macquarie

Street tomorrow, I could drop them off for you then.'

She had to listen, fuming, as they made their arrangements. And then it hit her. You went to see someone in Macquarie Street when your doctor could do no more for you.

'What's wrong with you?' she burst out.

'Nothing,' he said, looking amused. 'My son has rooms there.'

The people who have rooms there are specialists, she thought. He cannot have a son old enough — or can he? She did rapid mental arithmetic. The son must be at least in his thirties — that means he would have been born when Henry was only about twenty. She was suddenly seized with violent jealousy.

He was laughing at her. 'Now what?'

She wiped all expression from her face with the swiftness of an angry child attacking a blackboard with a duster.

★   ★   ★

No one had much to say on the drive to the city and out to Woollahra.

'Time to come in?' Janie asked when they reached her house. 'No? Well, see you tomorrow, Henry. And I'll ring you, Catherine. Bye, Andromeda.'

She laid a gentle finger on the cheek of the

195

sleeping Barnaby and stepped out of the car.

They all watched as she walked away.

'I like *her*!' Andromeda said with fervent warmth.

Henry said nothing but he might as well have done.

'Would you like to come and sit in the front now?' he asked over his shoulder, but whether he meant Catherine or Andromeda was not clear.

'We must not disturb Barnaby,' Catherine replied severely. 'Let's go.'

As the car sped along the back roads from the city to the Peninsula Andromeda's eyelids began to droop.

'Sea air,' Henry said, stealing a look through the car mirror. 'Wouldn't you like to drop off too?'

When you are spending precious time with someone important to you, you do not wish to 'drop off'.

'You are full of good ideas,' she said acidly.

He concentrated on the road.

★ ★ ★

The sun had slipped behind the hill when they drew into her drive. The house lay quiet in the shadows. She was grateful to see that Paul had not yet arrived; Barnaby's eyes flew open the minute the car engine stopped.

'Better get him fed,' Andromeda said, struggling out of the restraining harness and scooping him up before he could voice his annoyance. 'Thank you, Mr Green. I've had a lovely day.'

'My pleasure,' he said, smiling at her indulgently and giving her bottom a pat as she headed away to the house. Then he bent to help Catherine out of the car. 'Now you will be good, won't you?' he said.

'Good?'

'Your husband will come home tired and upset.'

The admonition in his tone enraged her. What sort of a bitch does he think I am?

'Did you have a lovely day too?' he asked, unperturbed by her tight face.

'I missed the children,' she flung at him.

If he thought her remiss as a wife he could not be allowed to think she was remiss as a mother.

It was not a lie. She *had* missed them. But the feeling had been one of relief, not loss. She had felt unencumbered and grateful. Now the way he was looking at her made her feel guilty.

Why had she ever thought him a comfortable man?

She pulled herself together. 'I'll just run in

and get Janie's things.'

'Make my apologies to your cat,' she said as she handed him the clothes. 'I have kept you away from him for too long.'

'Save them until you see him,' he retorted. And got into his car.

She stood and watched him drive away.

She felt sick with loss. She was afraid she might not see him or the bloody animal again.

As she stood there, limp and defeated, she heard the blare of a car horn and the sudden rasp of wheels biting the gravel.

It could only mean that his car and Peter's had come face to face in the drive. She fled into the house.

Pouring drinks was a two-handed job, she discovered, nevertheless she had two large glasses of whisky ready on the tray and her smile was warm and concerned as she indicated them to the two irritable men who erupted into the room.

'You must be so tired and upset,' she said.

Paul was beyond the comfort of Glenfiddich. 'Who the hell was that idiot?' he said.

18

'Simon . . . ?'

'He's fine.'

'And Jenny?'

'Fine too.' So don't make a fuss, his tone said.

He had been gone so short a space of time. She had known him so long. How could there be such distance between them?

Peter was jangling his car keys.

'Can't hang about. Lot of things to do and Miles will be wondering . . . '

Paul cut him short. 'Thanks for the lift. And . . . ' he poked his brother on the shoulder, 'remember she's on her own now. Don't leave it so long.'

'I know. I know.' Irritation was in the air.

Peter bent forwards to kiss Catherine goodbye.

He smelled fresh and looked so exquisitely clean that even the hairs in his nostrils shone gold.

'How did the thing go?' she began as they waved him goodbye and were walking back to the house.

'Be glad you weren't there.'

She looked up at him quickly. She had never seen him looking so strained. Paul was feeling grief.

If I knew him better I would feel it with him, she thought, but I can only feel my own sadness and leave him alone with his.

And he hasn't asked me about my arm, so he cannot feel my pain either. So what is to become of us?

She had no time to wonder further, for Andromeda had appeared and she found herself being ushered indoors.

'Put your feet up,' the girl said, pushing her down into the cushions of the great couch. 'You're the colour of putty.'

'Where's Barnaby?'

'On my bed. I've changed him and he's spark out.'

'He'll roll off!'

'Give me credit! He's got pillows all round him and my futon is on the floor.'

Ah, the futon, that example of Japanese masochism!

'He can sleep in his clothes for once,' Andromeda was going on, 'he'll only get cranky if we try to undress him. And he likes it in my bed.'

To Catherine this was heresy. A child should always sleep in fresh garments and in his own bed, unsullied by adult vapours.

'Oh, don't get awkward,' Andromeda said impatiently. 'And what about some food for Mr Grant? There's that cold watercress soup and I could do him an omelette.'

First she takes over my child, now my husband, Catherine thought, unable to feel the gratitude she knew she should. What use am I anyway?

'I knew you'd get upset,' Andromeda said. 'You did too much today and I bet that arm's giving you gyp. Would you like a nice big gin?'

'*Now* what is the matter?' Paul asked, suddenly materialising beside them, furrow-browed and looking down with distaste at his weeping wife.

'She's got a broken arm,' Andromeda said robustly, 'that's what's the matter. And there's more than enough to do round here when you've got two good ones.'

'Now then, now then,' he said so mildly that surprise halted Catherine in mid-sob. 'Just be a good girl and get me some food, will you?'

'She's seen to that. She's just told me to make you an omelette.'

'That would be very nice.'

'Like I did last time?'

'Certainly.'

Andromeda flashed a quick smile and was off. Paul turned to Catherine. His irritation seemed to have eased. 'Is it very painful?'

'No. Just frustrating.'

'Then don't try to do anything. The children are away. You can leave things to Andromeda. And why don't you go to bed now? There's nothing for you to do down here.'

There was not. There certainly was not.

She got up awkwardly. She would have to do without that nice big gin.

'Goodnight then.'

'Goodnight.'

Upstairs she crawled into her bed. Like Barnaby she would sleep in her clothes. But she could not sleep. It seemed a long time before the light from Andromeda's room lit her ceiling and the girl's voice floated up through her open window.

'I told you he was all right. Snug as a bug in a rug. Now you go and get some sleep; you must need it.'

She heard the murmur of Paul's reply and the crunch of his feet on the gravel. He had actually gone across to Andromeda's room with her to check on Barnaby. She listened for his step on the stairs. He ran up lightly and she heard the crisp click of his closing door. He did not check to see how she was. Henry Green would have done so. Wouldn't he? Or had he withdrawn from her too?

You are going to have to pull yourself together, Catherine, she told herself. And remember to take those bloody pills. All the reminders Henry Green had insisted upon had been of no avail. She would have to ask Andromeda to take charge. She seemed to have taken charge of everything else.

★   ★   ★

By the time she came downstairs the following morning Paul had left and there was peace in the kitchen.

'His appetite!' Andromeda said contentedly, spooning mashed banana and cornflakes into Barnaby. 'And just look at you! We'll have to do something about that hair.'

'It's too much to cope with. I'll have it cut off.'

'Don't be barmy! You won't need that sling for long. They'll just keep your arm in plaster. You'll soon be able to use it.'

Some people can be too damn cheerful. Let her try a left-handed sponge-down when the body is longing for submersion in warm, scented water and see how she feels.

'Tell you what,' Andromeda said, 'we've got a lovely free day. How about I shampoo your hair and give you a facial? And I could give you a rub-down. I've got some lovely oils.'

I hate people being *kind* to me, Catherine thought savagely, struggling to show gratitude, they are always so damned pleased with themselves.

'I'll do your nails and all,' Andromeda said, being ever so kind. 'Toes too.'

'How about a nice little colonic irrigation?'

'What?'

The young, puzzled face brought Henry Green's reproof sharply to mind.

Andromeda was not thick, just unaccustomed to sarcasm.

'Sorry,' she said, and meant it. 'I was being silly.'

'You've had enough to make you silly.'

Enough was enough. The girl was within a hair's-breadth of being patronising.

'Well don't just talk,' Catherine said briskly. 'Jump to it!'

⋆　⋆　⋆

By mid-afternoon she was shampooed, coiffed, manicured, pedicured and massaged, and feeling much better for it.

'That lilac eye shadow,' Andromeda said, inspecting her. 'Just a touch.'

A touch it was. The girl showed the same gift that turned her cooking into something special. She had a way with the 'touch'.

204

When the telephone rang Catherine answered in her most seductive voice.

When one knows one looks charming it is impossible to be other than charming.

'That Henry Green of yours!' Janie said.

'What about him?' The purr had quite gone from her voice.

Janie began to laugh.

'He brought my stuff to the office and I was on the phone so Eve had to deal with him. You know her! She's all for destroying every member of the male species! Well, blow me, the next thing I know they're arranging to have lunch together and off she goes at one o'clock and doesn't get back till half past three. All quiet smiles.'

'What did she say?'

'Sorry she was late.'

'That all?'

'Yes. But I do know they've exchanged telephone numbers.'

'Well, bully for Eve, and he's hardly 'my' Henry Green. He's only the man who got rid of the possums for me.'

'Well, he can get rid of my possums any time,' Janie said cheerfully. 'I think he's great. By the way, how was Paul when he got home?'

'Quiet. I think he really loved Ned.'

'You sound surprised.'

'Yes . . . Well . . . '

She could not waste sympathy on Paul.

If I died he would not grieve for me as he does for his father, she thought to herself. And why is he now so much easier with Andromeda than he is with me? That was a particularly uncomfortable thought to harbour and bred resentment against innocent parties.

'How's the arm?' Janie was enquiring.

'Not bad. Andromeda says I will soon be able to get rid of the sling.'

'Then let me know when you are fit enough to go and see Beth.'

'And you let me know how Eve makes out with Henry Green.'

They said laughing goodbyes. But Catherine did not feel amused. What the hell was Henry up to?

★   ★   ★

'I've gone Greek,' Andromeda exclaimed, planting a steaming bowl of soup on the dining-room table. 'I can't pronounce it.'

'Avgolemono,' Paul volunteered, sniffing and smiling. The lemon scent was fresh, the swirls of egg uncurdled and powdered cinnamon floated on the shining surface.

'And I've made do with everything I could

find for the rest. It's mostly veggies but the sauce is good. And we'll have to do some shopping tomorrow, we're clear out of . . . '

'Yes, yes,' Catherine interrupted her, her mind working quickly. 'You'll have to ring up Mr Green and see if he can drive us to the village again. I'm sure you'll find him in the book. Do it soon.'

Paul was quite uninterested in their domestic arrangements. His whole concern was for the wonderful flavour of the soup.

She certainly got it right, Catherine thought, noting with amused cynicism how Paul's attitude towards Andromeda had changed once her culinary creativity had become apparent. The route to the male heart was unquestioningly through the stomach. A natural athlete herself, she had felt impatience towards girls daunted by the vaulting horse and the impassioned flailing of the hockey field but who became all smiles as they donned their aprons for the cookery class. I was so damn clever I was allowed to substitute Studies of the Ancient World for cookery, a substitution that hardly prepares a girl for marriage.

'Sorry, darling, I burnt the dinner but would you like me to read you some *Beowulf* in the original?'

Paul looked up and caught her smiling.

'What?' he said.

'Nothing.'

He would see no humour in it. It was probably asking too much that he should. She was aware that he was aware of the improvement in her looks — the slight double-take had given him away — but he did not compliment her as he was now complimenting Andromeda.

'That was good,' he said.

The girl was all gratified smiles.

'Did Barnaby sleep well?' he asked.

'Till half past six. Then we played until it was time to get up.'

She made it sound like an idyll of happy childhood.

Paul obviously thought it was.

'Would you mind keeping him . . . ?' he asked, waving his hand towards Catherine, 'until . . . er . . . ?'

'Course I wouldn't. You couldn't expect her . . . '

'Fine,' he said, cutting her short. 'Now how about some coffee?'

'I'll bring it into the sitting room.'

Andromeda believed in gracious living. One did not relax after a meal with the wreck of it all around you; you left it behind for others to deal with and lay back in cushioned ease, sipping from tiny cups and nibbling small, expensive biscuits.

'There are coffee mugs on the dresser,' Catherine called out as she left the table. She was damned if she would allow herself to be dragooned by the upwardly mobile.

Andromeda got her own back by bringing in the tray bearing two large orange plastic mugs and the silver coffee pot.

'Let's see what else we can find,' Paul said, rising up and shooing Andromeda back to the kitchen. Incredibly he was smiling.

The moment was not quite right but was probably as near right as it would ever be, and Catherine was not built for caution.

'There is something we still haven't sorted out,' she said.

Paul, who was a cautious man, just inclined his head. 'Which particular something do you have in mind?'

'You know perfectly well. We can't go on living here. It's not a safe place for the children.'

He turned his cold gaze on her. 'Not again!' he said. 'I can't believe you. You know this house is all I ever dreamed of, is everything I worked for, and you want me to get rid of it because you are too idle to look after the children properly!'

'I'm not idle! That's unfair!'

'Forget it. We are not selling.'

'Even though the children could get hurt?'

'There you go! Do you call that fair?'

'It's fact.'

The expression on his face was unlike any she had seen him show before — it was incredulous, censorious and unforgiving.

'I really can't believe you, Catherine,' he said. 'I never dreamed you could turn out to be such a bitch.'

'I've rung Hen . . . that Mr Green about the shopping,' Andromeda said, suddenly appearing to collect the coffee cups. 'He's sorry but he's got something to do in the city tomorrow. But he says he's found the supermarket very good. If you ring them and tell them what you want they will deliver.'

'I do not shop solely at the supermarket,' Catherine said grandly. 'I will give my husband my list. I'm sure his secretary will be able to cope.'

'He said if you have any more trouble with the possum to let him know.'

'Oh, that chap,' Paul said, presenting a normal front to Andromeda, 'the ranger. I'd like to buy a couple of traps from him.'

'Well, you can't,' Catherine told him, 'he's not a ranger. He's H.G. who does the chess problems — and the cryptic crossword — in the daily paper.'

He became more normal than ever.

'H.G.? That fat chap who nearly wiped us out in the drive? H.G.? Well, I'd certainly like to talk to him!'

'He's hardly your type,' Catherine said bitingly.

'I doubt if you know what 'my type' is.' His tone was just as sharp.

'He's lovely,' Andromeda broke in. 'I'm sure he'd lend you his cages if you asked him. I've written his phone number on the pad.'

'I'll ring him then,' Paul said.

'O-ooh, Mrs Grant,' Andromeda said, 'you've gone that funny colour again. Is your arm hurting? Do you want me to help you to bed?'

'No! Certainly not. I can manage perfectly well.'

It was difficult to rise gracefully from the chair; the plastered arm lying heavy across her chest made for imbalance.

'Goodnight,' she said shortly.

For the second night in a row she retired unwashed and in her clothes and didn't give a damn. She was too occupied with the gnawing questions as to what Henry Green had to do that he considered more important than her call for help and why he was going to the city again tomorrow when he had only been there yesterday. And what was he going to think when he received Paul's telephone call? And why, most pressing question of all, had she not heard from him in the last few days?

19

'But she *depends* on it.' Andromeda had realised she could not leave Catherine over the weekend and go to stay in her room at Dulcie Tims' as she usually did.

'My rent! She *needs* it!'

'Then post it to her,' Catherine said, unable to understand the drama.

'Send money by *post*? I wouldn't dare! She says the postman would rather eat her letters than take them up there.'

Catherine's sympathies were with the postman.

'Then I'll give you a cheque for the money. You can send that.'

'She wouldn't have anything to do with a *cheque*! They might find out!'

That the authorities might discover she had a rental income and reduce her pension was a concern of Dulcie's with which Catherine had every sympathy. It matched her own refusal to allow Andromeda to declare her earnings as her helper. Such piddling amounts to the State, she thought, but making such a difference to the quality of life for some people.

'Would you be all right if I went over on the bus and took her the rent? I'd be as quick as I could.'

'Rubbish,' Catherine said. 'We'll all go! Take a taxi. Have an outing. I hate being stuck inside all day.'

'You couldn't go up to the house,' Andromeda said quickly, 'look what happened last time.'

'I wasn't planning to. You can do the mad scramble. Barnaby and I will wait in the taxi at the bottom of the . . . '

'*Would* you, oh, *would* you?'

'I've just said so, haven't I?'

All this high drama over so little was becoming irritating.

★   ★   ★

It was going to be a hot day. Small pearls of sweat already moustachioed Barnaby's top lip and everything was displeasing him. Andromeda was having difficulty getting his nappy on.

'Isn't he a love?' she said brightly to Catherine as she captured the flailing limbs and up-ended him by the ankles in order to place loud raspberry kisses on his bare bottom. The screams became shouts of joy.

'Never fails,' Andromeda said.

Hardly a universal panacea, Catherine thought acidly.

The girl looked at her sharply. 'Shall I ring for the taxi while you get changed?'

'Why should I get changed?' Though she had slept in the loose Indian-cotton dress it was nevertheless a dress and crumples were natural to it.

'But you're not wearing any . . . You can see . . . '

'For heaven's sake, I'll only be sitting in the taxi.'

'But the taxidriver . . . '

'Let's hope we make his day. Now tell me where I can find a rubber band. I've brushed my hair. All I need is something to hold it back.'

It was a modest enough need but one it proved impossible to satisfy.

'Oh, get me the scissors then,' Catherine said, exasperated beyond bearing.

'No! You can't!'

'Oh, yes I can.'

'I'm walking out that door if you do!'

Catherine frowned, unbelieving. 'Are you threatening me?'

'I don't know what I'm doing.' Tears were not far away. 'But you're awful talking like that. Just because things won't do what you want them to do! And you're *cruel*! Your hair is *beautiful* — some people would kill for it! How would you like it if you were stuck with mine?'

Their raised voices startled Barnaby out of his joyous delirium of naked freedom and he ceased waving his arms and legs and turned his head sharply, his eyebrows high and his smooth, almond-shaped lids disappearing as his eyes became round with alarm. As he drew in a deep breath Andromeda lunged forwards. 'Look out!' she cried. 'He's going to pee!'

And pee he did, in a swinging arc that sprayed both of them as he began to rock backwards and forwards in distress.

Andromeda scooped him up into her arms, cuddling, kissing, comforting, her distress as vocal as his.

It was too much. All Catherine could do was laugh at the sheer ludicrousness of it all. The wet patch on Andromeda's dress was getting bigger by the second, the soft cotton of her own dress clung, moist and uncomfortable across her chest. The laughter took hold and she could not stop it.

Andromeda raised her head and stared at her in amazement. 'Now what?'

Catherine leant forwards and ruffled the spiky hair, her good humour quite restored.

'Guess who's going to have to change her

216

dress too?' she said, and laughed again at Andromeda's squawk of exasperation.

It was mid-morning before they were cleansed and changed, the order for the supermarket compiled and arrangements made for its delivery, and they were ready to go out.

'We have to call at the veggie shop, the delicatessen and the health food place,' Catherine said to the taxidriver who pulled up. She had decided that involving Paul and his secretary in her shopping carried the possibility of problems she could do without.

The taxi smelled of armpits and stale cigarette smoke but at least the driver did not make a fuss about Andromeda travelling with Barnaby sitting on her knee.

'What happened to the other fella?' he asked when he saw the sling, but was otherwise kind and patient as he helped Catherine into his cab.

They took the road along the coast for a few miles before turning inland to make the steep climb up the hill to Dulcie's shack. It was as though the world were dropping away; ahead there was only sky. Down below the crinkled sea was spread like blue taffeta over the bay, and the curvature of the earth showed, clean and clear against the wide horizon. Looking back over her shoulder

Catherine became aware of how cramped she had allowed her life to become, how rigid its confines. As the distance from home grew she felt as though she could see that life through the wrong end of a telescope, small and insignificant, dwindling to a blur, a smudge, a nothing.

When was the last time I even went for a walk, she wondered, could stride out free, able to think my own thoughts and look — just look and feel part of the life around me? I used to be able to feel the earth breathing. And I used to listen. She remembered the small rustle of the unseen bird in the hedge, the soft clop of her feet in the dust of the lane, the silver whine of silence. English memories. All her years in Australia had not made her an Aussie.

And yet it is here all the important things have happened to me — successful career, marriage, children. She thought over the noisy helter-skelter of the busy years — the insistent voices — no time just to *be*.

They were nearing the top of the plateau.

'I love it up here,' Andromeda said, and 'O-ooh, look!'

A car was coming towards them. Catherine recognised it at once and her stomach lurched. Henry Green was driving. He was smiling down at his passenger as the two cars passed each other and was oblivious to Andromeda's frantic waves. 'Oh, blow!' she said. 'Now what about the rent? That was Dulcie with him.'

It was indeed — there was no mistaking the sunhat.

Catherine was without speech. She had asked for his help and he had pleaded inability, but he was perfectly able to drive up here, collect Dulcie Tims and take her out. And he had said he was going into the city. How could he bear to be seen out with that scarecrow of a woman? She couldn't be — could she? — wearing those awful sandshoes?

'I wonder where they are going?' Andromeda echoed. 'It must be somewhere special. She's wearing the costume she got married in and that only comes out on state occasions.'

The driver drew up the taxi in the stony patch where the road ended and the path up to the shack began.

'This do you?' he asked.

They didn't know what did them.

'I'll have a smoke while you sort yourselves out,' he said. 'Great view.'

Andromeda was jiggling Barnaby up and down to try to contain his excessive energy.

'I could take it up and put it in her tea caddy so she'd find it as soon as she got in,' she worried, 'but would you be able to manage him while I'm gone?'

Not in his present state of excitability she wouldn't, and there was no way she could allow the girl to make the gruelling scramble carrying him.

'Forget it,' Catherine said. 'If Henry Green is such a friend of hers he can collect it from you and take it to her.'

She could feel herself getting into a 'state' and that wouldn't do.

'Do you think,' she asked the driver with intimidating charm, 'that I might steal one of your cigarettes?'

'You certainly might, m'dear.'

'And you needn't look at me like that,' she said to Andromeda. 'I don't propose to make a habit of it.'

'I should hope not! Mr Green would have something to say about that!'

There were other things he was required to have something to say about. Her deep inhalation of smoke was a mistake; her body was now unused to nicotine.

'See!' Andromeda said with satisfaction, watching her gasp and choke.

'I never smoke around my kiddie,' the driver chipped in. 'The wife wouldn't like it.'

Her eyes streaming, Catherine made a dramatic gesture of chucking the cigarette out of the cab window.

'Satisfied?' she said to Andromeda.

'I'm sorry to have wasted your cigarette,' she said to the man. Nobody could accuse her of bad manners.

He was looking at his watch. 'OK,' he said, 'but I've got another fare booked, so could we get on?'

It would be nice if just one man could be tractable and not flaunt his own imperatives. Now Barnaby, that man in embryo, was making his all too clearly known.

'Sorry,' Andromeda said, struggling to hold him. 'He wants to blow your horn. If you'd just let him he'd shut up and we could be off.'

'Imagine if we'd had Simon and Jenny with us!' Andromeda said when they got home.

The reminder that her crowded and tethered lot was well-nigh inescapable was unwelcome. Catherine banged about flinging windows wide. The house, which had been closed up, smelled stale.

'But you've put the fans on,' Andromeda remonstrated, 'you don't need to open windows when fans are on!'

'I do,' said Catherine, wreaking one-handed violence on resistant catches.

'But you're letting the hot air in!'

'Yes!' she agreed, taking great lungfuls of

221

the heavy, sweet scent of murraya, whose white-starred bushes were reckless with blossom.

'The gardener's been,' she said, leaning out over the sill to admire the smooth striping of the lawns and raked neatness of the paths.

'Did you leave his money out for him?'

'No.'

She waited for Andromeda's pained sigh. She hadn't left it out last week either.

'We'll take it round to him,' she said defensively. She was in no mood for a lecture about how people depended on reliable payments.

Andromeda was unloading the big, colourful, thick, canvas shopping bags Catherine had made, doing her sewing machine no good in the process, in her effort to protect the environment against the despised and ubiquitous plastic. At least she can't pillory me about *those*, she thought.

The outing had not done much for Andromeda either.

'You would have thought the delicatessen would have had mascarpone,' she complained.

Catherine felt no such annoyance. She was content with what she called 'honest' cheese. With spring onions. Or pickled ones.

'It's so *versatile*,' the girl was moaning on.

Does handsprings and plays the guitar? Catherine wondered acidly. Reverent conversation about food got on her wick.

'I was going to make this thing — but it doesn't matter — if Mr Grant's not going to be home, it can wait.'

Catherine did not know Paul would not be home. He had obviously thought the information of more importance to Andromeda than to her.

Irritation was piling on irritation.

But Andromeda was cheering up.

'He was up real early. Came across and sat with Barnaby. He wanted that blue shirt but it was at the cleaners so I ironed him the one with the pale blue stripes . . . '

'Isn't that the telephone?' Catherine asked, grateful she could escape before she did damage.

'I thought you would like to know,' Janie's amused voice said. 'Eve has taken the day off. She wouldn't tell me why but has promised to fill me in later. What's the betting it has something to do with your Henry Green?'

'You'd lose your money. He's out with somebody else.'

'One hell of a ladies' man, isn't he?' Janie said admiringly.

She was in no mood for chat.

'I have to go. Barnaby is playing up,' she lied.

'Then I'll keep you posted.'

★ ★ ★

There was no way she would wait to be 'posted'.

When Andromeda took Barnaby down to her room to put him to bed she made a telephone call.

'Catherine?' the surprised voice said.

'I want to go for a walk,' she stated, without preamble. 'I *need* to go for a walk. Will you take me?'

'When?' he said, slow and careful.

'Tonight. Can you be at the end of the drive at nine o'clock?'

He was in no hurry about that either.

'Very well,' he said at last.

Don't burst with enthusiasm, she said to herself, and was about to speak again, when the machine clicked.

No matter. She would soon be seeing him.

Dulcie Tims. That receptionist of Janie's.

I can deal with *them*, she thought. They don't know the Henry I know. The thought of seeing him, never far from her mind, now lay like velvet over the sorenesses of the day.

224

20

'Barnaby's got a red spot on his cheek and he's grinding his gums,' Andromeda announced. 'I'll have to lie with him to get him off. There are biscuits and three lots of my dip if you get hungry.'

Her dips were delicious, as Catherine, a garlic-lover, well knew, but this was no time for them. One did not have garlic breath when with a loved one in the confines of a car.

'Don't bother about me,' she said. 'Just stay with Barnaby.'

'No dinner?'

'Not for me.'

'Then I'll just make do with apples and cheese. See you in the morning.'

Everything was working out well. Her perfumed departure from the house would go unobserved.

★　★　★

He did not come in his car. As she arrived at the end of the drive and leant against the smooth trunk of the scribbly gum to regain her breath she heard the crunch of feet approaching. He was even more out of breath than she was. His face was part of the warm dark, his bulk a deeper shadow against the shadows. She felt her nipples stiffen.

'Ill met by moonlight?' she asked mischievously.

'Only there's no ruddy moon.'

His breathing was ragged; mischievous was not his mood of the moment.

'I thought you would come in the car.'

'I don't drive in the dark. I have poor night vision.'

She had barely time to feel gratification that he should have been willing to walk up to see her when he said, 'I hadn't realised it would seem so damn far. I hope you don't want to . . . '

'No, no,' she said hastily, 'there's a reserve just along the road. We can sit down comfortably there.'

She led the way to the reserve, which lay back from the road and tucked beneath the brow of the escarpment. Stumbling in the dark they discovered the table and bench supplied for those who wished to picnic or use the barbecue. The rich, greasy smell of recently cooked food thickened the night air.

He sank down on the wooden bench with a sigh of relief. As she sat beside him she realised her promise of comfort would not be met.

'Why?' he asked with what breath he had left.

It was time to be winsome.

She arranged herself beside him so that her damaged arm would not prevent him from embracing her.

'I felt a *need*,' she replied. 'People just walk these days, all set-jawed and bent on doing themselves good, not a bit like it used to be when you wandered, gentle, aimless, feeling free, aware of space . . . '

'Was that your need? Space and freedom?'

'Yes. A need I felt badly.'

'It is wise to put feelings under close scrutiny,' he said.

She waited but he showed no indication of further interest in hers. She did not know what to say next.

She looked up into the wide, dark-blue sky, prickly with stars. There were no patterns she could recognise. The Plough? Where is Orion? Where Betelgeuse? She felt abandoned by familiar friends. I am under strange skies, she thought, and shivered.

A car whooshed past on the road below. As its lights and sound faded he seemed to be pulling himself together.

'How is your arm?' he asked.

Thank God he was sounding like himself again.

'Coming along. I think I could do without the sling now. Will you untie it for me?'

She half turned her back and lifted her hair so that he could reach the knot in the silk scarf she had insisted on using as a sling. The knot was tight. He could barely see what he was doing. As he fumbled and bent close she felt his breath on her neck. It was all she could do to prevent herself from turning.

'There,' he said. The knot was undone and the sling slipped free.

Her plastered arm was heavy but mobile.

'My fingers feel stiff.'

He took her hand and began to massage them, dealing with each one slowly and devotedly. She closed her eyes and gave herself up to the communication she remembered so well. The flux of energy was subtle, but intense, impersonal yet personal.

When he gave her hand back to her he kissed it.

She sat bemused.

'Now see how you go,' he instructed her.

She went well. She curved and uncurved her fingers, lifted her arm and smoothed her hair, made royal movements to imaginary milling crowds. There was no reason now — surely — for him not to take her in his arms.

He eased himself upright. The difficulty of

adapting his bulk to the harsh inhospitality of the bench was clearly a problem.

'Is your husband back?' he asked when he had disposed his limbs as comfortably as possible.

'Yes.'

'How is he?'

'Hostile. He refuses to consider selling the house.'

'I didn't mean . . . '

She realised, too late, what he did mean.

'He's upset,' she said, showing a proper concern, 'poor man. He's taking it hard. I suppose you could say that — in his own way — he is suffering.'

'And what is his own way?'

'How do I know?'

And that wasn't the right answer either.

Suddenly remembering, she said, 'By the way, you will be getting a telephone call from him. Don't worry — it's only about possum cages. He would like to borrow them. I knew you wouldn't mind. I can always rely on you, can't I?'

Bad moves were coming naturally to her.

His face was impassive. 'Any time,' he said.

It was more than wise to change tack.

'Thank you for your tip about the supermarket,' she said warmly. '*What* a help that was.'

'I'm glad. I'm sorry I couldn't . . . '

'Don't worry about it! First things are first after all and some things are much more important than others.' Wisdom had no defence against rabid curiosity. 'How did you spend your day?'

And bugger it, she thought, I can't do with pussyfooting around no matter how wise it may be.

'I know who you were *with*, but I don't know why and I don't know where you went.'

'Is that another of your needs — always to know?'

She made no reply. She knew when honesty was not the best policy. But she could not keep it up.

'I can't believe you would prefer to be with that creature . . . '

'Dulcie Tims,' he corrected.

'I know! The female version of Neanderthal man!'

She could not tell whether his involuntary snort was of amusement or anger. It was time to forget about Dulcie Tims.

'Oh, Henry,' she said softly, 'I was *so* disappointed. We had the chance of time together. I thought you would . . . '

'Arrangements had been made. I could not go back on them.'

'I would have,' she said.

He was rubbing his chest with his clenched fist.

'Please,' he said, 'dear girl — could we leave it? It's been a tiring day.'

And whose fault is that, she was about to retort, when she realised he was in pain.

'What's wrong?'

'Just a touch of indigestion.'

She instantly began to rummage in her bag. Pregnancies had made the indigestion tablet a constant companion. Thankfully she could now use both hands.

She unwrapped two of the tablets, placed them on her palm, and raised her hand to his mouth.

'Take these.'

The warm touch of his searching lips brought on a wave of exasperation. It was all such a waste of time.

He sat with his shoulders hunched and continued to rub his chest.

As she watched him, panic suddenly struck her in the belly.

It had been an irksomely hot day; he had made the long drive into the city, spent time there, and had to face the long drive back; and then — when he probably felt the need for a rest — had made the gruelling walk from his place down by the sea, up to the village and then the steeper, longer pull up to her house. And he was not built for it! The strain of carrying all that bulk! She had read about people who died from a heart attack they thought to be indigestion!

'Oh, my dear!' she cried, and flung her arms around him. 'Is the pain bad?'

'So.'

That meant it was awful.

The panic she felt when one of the children became ill engulfed her. Oh, God — no! please God — no!

As though in answer to her call came the reminder that there was a telephone box further along the road. She sprang up.

'Sit there!' she said urgently. 'Don't move! I'm going to call a taxi! We must get you to hospital!'

'No!' he said, 'there is no need.'

For her there was every need.

'I won't be long,' she said, leaning down to pat his face as she turned to go, but he clutched at her.

'I know what's best,' she cried, wrenching herself free.

He made a sudden lunge to bar her path, and as he did so his body gave vent to a long, explosive, reverberating belch. She heard his stomach rumbling like a train gathering speed to leave a station.

He sagged on the bench and took long, uneven breaths.

'Sorry about that,' he said.

She had seldom been so glad about anything. Weak his stomach might be but his heart was sound. She both collapsed with relief and soared with gratitude.

'Oh, God,' she said, 'I thought . . . '

Her arms were round him, her lips pressed to the soft flesh of his scarred cheek.

'You're a great one for jumping to conclusions, aren't you?' he said, sounding tired to death.

At least he was in no danger. But the evening was ruined. She had sense enough to know when to cut her losses.

She kissed him on the forehead. 'I'm not letting you walk home,' she said. 'I'll go and call that taxi.'

He did not argue.

★　★　★

'Hello-hello,' the taxidriver chortled. 'I didn't expect to see you again so soon!'

And certainly not up here, at this time of night, his expression said.

Catherine helped Henry into his seat without replying.

'Goodnight, Mr Green,' she said with

polite formality. 'It was very good of you to come. I'm sure my husband will be pleased to see you again next week.'

'Night, love,' the cabbie said, though he might as well have said 'Pull the other one.'

As she plodded, disappointed, back along the road home she looked down to where the lights of the village twinkled between the trees and the invisible sea made a low, rhythmic rustle. She had seldom felt more alone or felt the vastness of the alien sky more empty.

★   ★   ★

When she turned into the drive she was startled to see lights blazing from the house windows. Heart in mouth she began to run.

Paul was patrolling up and down the kitchen with a weeping Barnaby in his arms. Andromeda was frantically searching through the cupboards.

They both turned and glared at her, allies and companions-in-arms.

'Where have you been?' Andromeda accused. 'His tooth's giving him gyp and I'd nothing over there to give him. I came to see if you've got any baby Panadol.'

'I didn't think you were coming home,' Catherine said apologetically to Paul. 'I went for a walk.'

234

'Find the medicine,' he replied, his eyes cold with condemnation.

'What have you done with your sling?' Andromeda demanded.

She found the aspirin.

★   ★   ★

It was impossible to sleep.

She saw herself too clearly through Paul's eyes. Useless, unreliable. As I suppose I am, she conceded.

But I can't be all that bad!

When I thought Henry was having a heart attack I didn't worry about myself and what might happen if there were the drama of an ambulance and questions asked as to what we were doing up there — all I thought about was him. And that's hardly an argument I could put to Paul to make him think better of me.

And whatever must Henry think?

Making a fuss about that damn woman was downright stupid.

Arrangements had been made, he said. Knowing him he would be too tender-hearted to break them. He was probably taking her to have her bunions done, or on some other delicate little matter. That's all it was.

That's all it could have been.

I must see him tomorrow to find out how he is and I will apologise. Mend my fences. He will see how douce and pleasant I can be. He will forgive me. On the edge of sleep she thought she heard Barnaby crying again but the sound was too faint to make her lift her head — and anyway, Andromeda was there. She did not see the shadows on the ceiling as the light in Andromeda's room came on, nor hear the swift footsteps across the grass and then the murmur of concerned voices.

21

Barnaby's tooth was through, he was again good-tempered and boisterous.

'Kill you before they die themselves,' said Andromeda, the surrogate mother. She certainly looked wan.

'You must go back to bed when he has his morning sleep,' Catherine told her.

Paul had left before they rose, apparently unfed, for there were no dishes to prove otherwise. Typical, Catherine thought savagely, aware that even now his secretary would be rushing about and buttering bagels.

She looked at her watch. Too early to ring Henry. It would have to wait until Andromeda and Barnaby slept.

'You're not going to be silly now that you've taken your sling off, are you?' she was being questioned.

'I will be able to drive now. The plaster is quite comfortable.'

Andromeda groaned.

She was sitting at the table, Barnaby in his highchair at her side, a pile of fresh green beans in front of them.

'Do you think you could slice these?'

No, of course she couldn't. The plaster was heavy; how could she hold up her arm for a fiddly job like that?

'Cook them whole,' she said.

Andromeda gave Barnaby a bean to chew and picked up a knife.

Ah well, if she wanted to make a martyr of herself.

Catherine drifted through into the sitting room and looked at her watch again. I know, she thought suddenly, I'll ring Janie. She said she'd keep me posted about that girl of hers.

Janie's number was engaged. Ten minutes later it still was. And ten minutes later.

* * *

In Janie's office she and Eve were sitting together. The phone was off the hook.

'Go on!' said Janie, fascinated and letting her coffee grow cold in the cup.

Eve's small, dark face was unusually animated.

'When he said he was having lunch with his son and would I like to join them I said yes, please! Straight off. Just like that. And you know me! But he's so easy to talk to — ten minutes with him and I was telling him things I don't even tell you.'

'What sort of things?'

238

'About Millie.'

For Janie, Millie was the constant unseen presence, the dying sister to whom Eve's life was dedicated.

'I said that watching someone you love die sharpened your critical attitudes — made you angry with people — 'And very tired,' he said. 'My wife had cancer.' And we looked at each other. And, oh, Janie, I can't tell you how I felt. Suddenly there was somebody besides me — somebody who *knew*.'

'Yes ... well ... ' Janie stumbled, conscious of her own limitations. 'What was his son like?'

'Gorgeous. Totally drop-dead. You could see what his father was like when he was young.'

'What is he doing in Macquarie Street?'

'Working with an oncologist. He's doing research.'

He isn't looking for people to practise on? Janie worried. Aloud she said, 'Where did he take you for lunch?'

'The Botanical Gardens. He'd brought a big basket — sandwiches, cheese and fruit — and great big tea towels to tuck in. You should have seen us. It was like a teenage party. But all the time I had the feeling he was watching me, weighing me up ... '

'What about the son?'

'Apparently Henry had just said he was bringing a friend and left it at that, and you could see Andrew — that's his name — wondering if I was — you know — and being amused and Henry, knowing what he was wondering, and being amused too.'

'And where did all this amusement get you?'

'He told Andrew he just wanted us to say hello to each other for now. 'She has a problem we might help her with,' he said, 'you could have information, know a special man.'

' 'Ah,' Andrew said and gave me such a lovely look.

' 'Not me, my sister!' I said, and relief came all over his face. Henry said perhaps we could have a bit of time together soon. Would he like to spend a weekend? And he said 'You bet. Tee it up, Dad. It's time I paid my respects to Tom anyway.' Who's Tom?'

'The cat,' said Janie wickedly, knowing Eve's weakness for felines. 'So, a good time is about to be had by all!'

'Not only that. Andrew had to go back to work and we sat on. Henry was still giving me this considering look. 'What?' I said.

'It seems there is this woman. He says she was a great help to him and his wife. I asked what sort of help, and he hesitated.

' 'Look,' I said, 'we've tried everything and I'm still looking — it doesn't matter how outlandish it sounds — if there is any chance . . . ' 'She's different,' he said.

'Well, to cut a long story short, he took me to meet her yesterday.'

'So *that's* where you were!'

Eve leant back in her chair and blew her fringe up from her forehead.

'He wasn't wrong! Different isn't the word for it.'

'Get on with it, will you?'

'I said the lunch would be on me and I arranged the place and time. Lovely little restaurant, down by the water. My local. I got there first and when I was looking through the window saw them getting out of his car. A great hulk of a woman, wearing a sunhat and a suit that *gripped*. I rushed over to a table in an alcove, looking out over the bay. I hoped we couldn't be seen there! He brought her in and thanked me for choosing such a delightful place with such a lovely view and looked straight at me. And, Janie, it was as though he were challenging me, not the sort of look you take lightly.

' 'This is my newest friend, Eve, and this is Dulcie, one of my oldest ones,' he said. She cocked an eye at me. 'Going in for looks now, are you?' she said. He got her seated as

241

though she were royalty, took charge of the tatty hold-all she was carrying and there we were. What a one-off! She looks like — I can't tell you — but she doesn't give a damn. She knows who she is.

'He told her that I worked for you, and that you were a friend of the Mrs Grant her lodger helps out. 'God Almighty,' she said, 'life doesn't half throw nets round people. Where's the menu?' It was a work of art.

'She clicked her tongue at the waiter.

' 'That's all very well,' she said, 'but what's the cooking like?'

'It was good.

' 'Tell the lad in the kitchen he's done well,' she told the bemused waiter at the end of the meal.

' 'Coming from Mrs Tims that is a compliment to treasure,' Henry said wickedly.

'Oh, Janie, I'd like to have been in the kitchen when the waiter got back there. Nothing was said about why Henry wanted us to meet. It didn't seem as though he'd told her. We sat over coffee and looked out over the water and at the rich people's big white houses and the expensive boats, gleaming and bobbing. You could see clear across to the Bridge.

' 'A million-dollar view,' I said. 'Flash,' she retorted scornfully. 'I could show you a real view.' Henry excused himself to go to the loo.

'I could feel she was staring at me but I couldn't smile back. If I looked like her I wouldn't want anybody to even see me. Her face is so parched by the sun her skin is like crumpled, grubby chamois leather.

' 'Hey,' she said.

'So I did look at her, and honestly, Janie, I came up in goosebumps.

' 'Don't hang on so tight, love,' she said. 'You're doing it for *you*. Be kind to her — let her go.'

'I couldn't speak. I went wobbly as a jelly. All I could do was stare, and I think that face is printed on my mind for the rest of my life. That's what Millie has been saying. 'I'm so tired. Let me go.'

'Then she patted my hand, picked up her hold-all and started ferreting about in it. 'Never a bloody pencil when you want one,' she said. 'Where's that waiter? That fish sauce was good. I'd like the recipe for it.'

'And then Henry came back and took me home and went off with her somewhere. Boy! What a day!'

'What does Henry say about all this?'

'I haven't been able to get hold of him. When I rang him last night he wasn't there.'

'And how do you feel now?'

'I dunno. The thought of losing Millie still

freaks me out, but . . . '

She looked up at Janie, her face wet with tears. 'But, oh, I can't tell you how good it is to know he's *there*. He's been through it — he knows . . . '

'And he'll be there as long as you need him, I don't doubt,' Janie comforted her.

'I didn't know there were any men like him — or Andrew.'

'Well there you are! Prejudices of a lifetime blown out of the water. Come on now, mop up! You're not the girl for tears!'

She stood up and dropped a quick kiss on the dark, dishevelled head. 'Though there are others who will be if I don't put the phone back on again.'

'You turned it *off*!'

'You don't think I'd let anything disrupt my hearing about all that, do you?'

Shock and disapproval transformed the tear-streaked face.

'Well put it back on again!'

Mopping up was swift.

Eve was not one to let the clients down.

22

Time was passing all too slowly for Catherine.

She went back into the kitchen.

'Isn't it time you put him down?' she asked Andromeda.

'The beans,' Andromeda said severely, 'and it isn't half past eleven yet.'

The telephone in the sitting room was ringing.

It was him!

Charm enveloped her like a cloak.

'I am *so* glad — I was wondering . . . ' she began but he cut in.

'Could you come down to the house this morning? Leave Barnaby with Andromeda? I'll send a taxi for you.'

'I will *walk*,' she cried, anxious to prove that she too could suffer in the name of love.

She was alight with joy. He wanted to see her. Last night he had been unwell; today he was himself again. And he had *invited* her to his house. She no longer had to scheme how to be privy to the intimacies of his life.

'I'd like to go for a walk,' she told Andromeda. 'It's so wonderful to feel free,' and swung her plastered arm to demonstrate.

'You and your walks,' Andromeda said indulgently, obviously bearing no ill will for last night's debacle.

Catherine rang Beth to check on Simon and Jenny before she left.

'I'm glad you're feeling better,' the kind voice replied, 'and don't worry about the children — or me — we're having a lovely time. Don't feel guilty for a minute. You need the rest and I need the distraction, so it's worked out well for everybody.'

It had indeed.

Her gratitude to Beth was boundless — and to Andromeda, who accepted delegation so willingly and honoured it so scrupulously.

'It's hot out,' the girl was saying. 'You ought to wear a hat. What about the one you bought for the funeral?'

I am not going to a funeral and I will not wear the hat, Catherine thought. Large-brimmed hats inhibit the embrace.

★ ★ ★

When she opened the gate in the tall brushwood fence she felt like a child entering tom tiddler's ground, delightedly looking for gold and silver.

And here it was.

The lawns were wide (he must have a ride-on mower). Bushes — hibiscus, grevillea, frangipani — and trees — ghost gum, pepper — enclosed the garden. Sheep may safely graze, she thought joyfully. A large, brown, wooden house sprawled across the block, the great windows winking in the sun like watchful eyes.

It was all he had said she needed.

She drew in a deep breath.

His house.

Her mind was working furiously. Possibilities spilling out like precious coin. His big, black cat came stalking out from the shrubbery, his tail erect as a walking-stick.

'Hello, Tom,' she said winningly. She was not going to repeat her past mistakes. The slitted eyes remained inimical. Don't Tom me, they said as he made his stately way past her.

'Going for his constitutional,' Henry said, emerging from the house and looking larger than ever.

'You really are better,' she said. 'You had me so worried.'

'You were very sweet.'

They were getting off to a good start.

'Come along in,' he said, putting a hand on her shoulder and guiding her to the open door in the great plate-glass window.

The room was part sunlight, part shadow. It ran back from the striped brilliance of bare, polished wood to the soft dimness of deep, cushioned couches and the glint of picture glass on the far walls. It was big. The couches were big. The pictures were like quiet windows into another world.

'Oh,' she said. This was nothing less than rapture.

He eased her into one of the couches. 'Sit down. Put your feet up. Drink?'

She heard the clink of bottle and glass, the slight fizz of the tonic and the reassuring plop of the lemon slice. What was gin and tonic without it?

He brought the glass to her. She was expecting him to sit beside her, for there was plenty of room, but he moved over to one of the other couches.

'Hey!' she chided. 'I won't be able to hear you over there. And I can barely see you!'

'S-ssh,' he said. 'You've had a tiring walk.'

She had. And it had all been downhill. Last night he had taken the hard climb upwards.

'Are you sure you're . . . ?'

'S-ssh.'

She surrendered to the nurturing bossiness and bent her head to her glass. He mixed a powerful potion. Paul was mean with gin and

248

liberal with tonic as though the quenching of the thirst was the object of the exercise.

She drank deeply. This was no time for the leisurely sip. She could enjoy gin and tonic whenever she wished; there were better things to do with time now.

Soon her glass was empty.

'There,' she said, getting up and going across to him, and holding it out. He could have taken her hand and pulled her down beside him — after all he had *asked* her to come — but he struggled up from the depths of the chair.

'I'll vow this furniture has developed suction,' he said, and took the glass from her.

She did not smile.

'Another?'

'No, thank you.'

She looked around.

'You have a very big house,' she said.

'There were a lot of us.'

But no longer, she thought.

'Oh, sorry. Would you like . . . ?' he asked belatedly.

She indicated that she would.

There were five bedrooms, four of them larger than her own; bathrooms that could be tramped around; and a kitchen big enough and charming enough to make a dining room redundant. They came to an archway.

'That is my wife's part of the house,' he said.

Surely he meant 'was'.

Whatever he meant he turned her away.

'The garden?' he said.

He led her out into the bright sunlight to a wooden seat under a tree with too many low branches. Twigs caught at her hair. As she sat down he leant over and brushed the loose strands from her forehead. The gesture was affectionate.

'Thank you,' she said, touched, 'and thank you for inviting me here. I so wanted to see where you live so that when I don't see you I can imagine — otherwise you go off — are lost . . .'

'Do you like the house?'

'I love it.'

'You must bring the children. When do they get back?'

'Not yet.'

There was much to be decided before they returned.

She took her courage in both hands.

'I have been thinking,' she said. 'I have done what you said, put my feelings under close scrutiny.'

'And?'

'I cannot spend the rest of my life in a relationship that has gone so wrong. Oh,

Henry,' she burst out. 'It's so simple. This house is much too big for you now. Think how wonderful it would be if we shared it! I have enough money to pay for any recon-struction needed . . . '

'Hold it!' he said.

The words shot out, hard as a blow.

He turned his back and walked away from her, running his hand through his hair.

She began to feel afraid.

He collected himself and came back to face her.

'Why do you think I asked you to come here today?'

'To make up for last night.'

'To say what I intended to say — but was prevented.'

Now she really was afraid.

'I was going to tell you about Dulcie Tims . . . '

Relief flooded in. 'Oh,' she cried, 'is that all? Don't worry about that! I've quite forgiven you.'

'No, Catherine,' he said, 'it is not all.'

She had never seen him look so grave.

'Dulcie,' he said, 'has — talents. Talents not given to many of us.'

She hadn't a clue what he meant.

'And,' he went on, 'since she was chosen to have them and we were not, it surely follows that she is deserving of respect. Yes?

'Dulcie *sees*,' he continued.

Sees what, for God's sake?

She vaguely remembered that Andromeda had said that people came to her for help but the idea had seemed so unlikely as to be ludicrous. Was he meaning she was one of the 'bubble-bubble-toil-and-trouble' sisterhood? She certainly looked like one.

'I don't understand you.'

'I doubted if you could.'

There was an unhappy silence.

'I ask you to believe,' he went on at last, 'that Dulcie's wisdom helped my wife and me through our bad times.'

He might ask but it was ridiculous to expect her to believe.

Dulcie was a ratbag, an uneducated, charmless, loud-mouthed peasant who probably couldn't even spell wisdom.

'And I don't like your ignorant mockery of her.'

She bridled. Was he actually calling *her* ignorant?

He was studying her face. 'There's no point in going on with this, is there? We can each only speak as we have found.'

He didn't seem to think she had found very much at all.

But there was one thing she would find out.

'Where did you go with her yesterday?' she asked.

'I took her to see a girl I thought in need of her help.'

Everything suddenly fell into place. 'You mean that secretary of Janie's,' she flashed.

'Eve. Yes.'

He looked at her even more closely. 'Does that satisfy your need to know?'

It was all going horribly wrong.

'Oh, Henry,' she said, and tears began to slip down.

'Oh, Catherine,' he said, in a sad, vexed voice.

The tear-stained face she turned up to him was soft, smiling and crafty.

'I am your Humpty-Dumpty girl and you are putting me together again,' she said, hoping to make him smile too, 'and we will . . . '

'No!' he said quickly. 'You mustn't think that. That is what I wanted to say to you. There is no 'we'.'

'But there *is*!' she burst out. 'And you know it. The massage. You wanted me as much as I wanted you.'

He looked at her squarely. 'I don't deny it. I am only human. But I do not forget — as I wish you would not — that you are married and have children.' The dark eyes were cold.

'What you said about the house is unthinkable.' Distate twisted his mouth. 'Catherine — this was *her* home. My wife's. Surely you must see that.'

Belatedly she did. The sickness of shame swept over her.

'What you must think of me,' she muttered. 'I'm sorry — I'm so sorry.'

So this is what it feels like when the sky falls, she thought, when all is dust and chaos.

When at last she dared to look up at him she found only kindness in his face. Kindness that kills.

He gave her his handkerchief. She wiped her tears.

He took a deep breath. 'Now to the important thing,' he said, 'your marriage . . . You talk of ending it when you've barely given it a chance. No wonder I show concern for you.'

In spite of her misery she was stung.

'Five years and all I have been through!'

'And what have you? Loss of pride? Loss of self-love? That's kindergarten stuff. Hardly enough to throw aside a commitment and admit defeat. And remember, children can get lost in space and freedom.'

'You're cruel!'

'No. But sometimes one has to use strong medicine.'

'I should have remembered you were a vet,' she said bitterly.

He put his hand on her shoulder. 'No more fighting. Come back inside and sit down and let me mix you another drink.'

She resisted the gentle pressure. Wild horses could not have dragged her back in there.

Then he tipped her chin up. 'Come on now. Stop thinking of this as being the end. Make it the beginning.'

'Of what?'

'Your marriage.'

'H-mmphh! It takes two.'

'Does he want to break up?'

'How do I know? I know no more of what he thinks than he does of what I do.'

'Then find out. It's only been five years after all. You're only just breaking each other in.'

'Spare me your homilies!'

'Try,' he persisted. 'Promise me. You haven't run out of chances yet.'

She felt as though she had run out of everything.

'What am I going to do without you?' she asked miserably.

'You won't be without me. I am still your good friend.'

That was the trouble. He was good friend to all the world and she had wanted more than that from him. She had wanted exclusive rights. The strength of her possessiveness had been surprising. She had never felt it in any other of her relationships — even with Paul.

'I have never *needed* anyone before.'

'And you mustn't need me now. I told you before — you'll only find real safety in yourself.'

'Another bloody homily!

'I am right about you, you know,' she went on. 'You may have retired but you're still the vet. Can't resist sick animals, can you? Or is it a kiss-and-make-better complex?'

He laughed and took her in his arms. He kissed her. A great, long, parting kiss.

'Time to go home,' he said.

He called a taxi.

★   ★   ★

Nadir, she thought as she lay back in the cab.

The lowest point. A word often used in crossword puzzles.

And that is where he flung me, without compunction.

Define compunction.

Regret for causing pain.

Of all people in the world I would have thought him the least likely to be willing to cause anyone pain, but there was no hesitation.

Bang, bang. You're dead.

Andromeda was right. I should have worn my funeral hat.

★ ★ ★

When she got home Andromeda greeted her exuberantly.

'I'd got it mixed up!' she said. 'It wasn't mascarpone I wanted, it was mozzarella. It says in the book you eat mascarpone with fruit and sugar and here was me going to do it with olive oil and basil.'

Catherine brushed her aside.

'I'm going to have a bath.'

'The plaster!'

'I'll rest it on the soap rack, and I don't want any help. Concentrate on your bloody cheeses.'

'Oh, poor you. You must be feeling rotten. All this walking does you no good at all. But you won't be told, will you?'

Catherine tried to ignore the infuriating, loving scolding but Andromeda clucked on.

'I'd go straight to bed afterwards, if I was

you. I'll tell Mr Grant you're feeling poorly.'

And would Mr Grant care?

As she hauled herself up the wide staircase she was biting her lip so hard she tasted blood.

23

'Cat!'

She looked up in shock to find Paul standing and staring down at her.

'What are you doing? Don't you know how long you've been in here? Andromeda is worried.'

She felt ridiculously embarrassed. Her clothes were strewn about the bathroom floor, her hair was falling about her face. She sank lower in the water to conceal her nakedness from him.

'Aw, come on!' he said. 'Show some sense. Get out for heaven's sake.'

He looked round for towels.

Gritting her teeth she reached up for the handle in the tiles by which to pull herself up, but it was high and her plastered arm made her clumsy.

He clicked his tongue. 'I suppose I'll . . . '

He had to screw himself around to get his hands under her armpits. 'Now!'

She came up with a whoosh and a squelch, water slopping all over the sleeves of his cashmere sweater.

'Sorry,' she said, 'I'm sorry.'

He snatched up towels. 'Here.'

She tried ineffectually to drape herself in them and blundered past him into the bedroom.

He followed her in, wiping the water from his sleeves. It seemed a long time since they had been in the room together. He let her get into bed then sat down at the bottom of it.

'Five minutes more and Andromeda would have been calling Police Rescue. Whatever were you thinking of?'

'Nothing I could tell *you*,' she said savagely.

There he sat, his fine, clear features as handsome as ever. No sag, no bloat for Paul. He was wearing, with elegance, his polo-necked cashmere sweater and finely checked trousers of impeccable cut — the image of taste and style.

He shook his head at her. 'I don't understand you. I don't seem to know you any more.'

Her ready temper flared. 'Of course you don't! I don't know me either!'

'But . . . ' he said, bewildered.

It all poured out then, white hot.

'Think about it! Three children in three years before I'd even had a chance to learn to be a mother! It comes naturally to some women — but not to me! As a mother I make a damn good journalist! It's bad enough having to cope with that failure — but have you noticed how my body has changed? Of course you bloody have! And I have to cope with your distaste for it as well as my own.'

He attempted to speak but she shut him up roughly.

'Do you know what it's like to feel utterly defeated — and tired — so bone-weary you can't even bother to wash?'

'You should have told me,' he said, visibly shocked.

'You should have known! And you wouldn't have listened anyway.'

'You're making sure I do now.'

'Yes . . . well . . . ' she said and burst into tears.

'Oh, Ca-at!'

He came across to the bed and attempted to put his arm round her but she wrenched away. It was not his arms she wanted.

She lay sobbing as he began to pace the room.

She needed a tissue so badly she could hardly breathe. Any minute she would have to blow her nose on the sheet. She sat up and groped for the box on her bedside table. It wasn't there.

With a sigh of irritation he gave her his handkerchief.

'Oh, Cat . . . ' he said. 'What am I going to do with you?'

There was weariness in his exasperation.

'I don't know. I don't know what to do with myself.'

'Well, we can't go on like this.'

'No.'

This is it, she thought, this is the watershed, and plunged on. 'I don't think we can go on at all.'

The sudden change in his expression startled her.

'What?'

She said, less strongly, 'I don't think we can go on together.'

He closed his eyes and began to rub his forehead. 'You're unbelievable, you really are. Do you know what you are saying?'

'Yes.'

'No, you don't. You haven't *thought*.'

'I've done nothing else but think.'

'About the children? Have you thought about them?'

'This is about them.'

'No, it isn't. It's about the house! You'd do anything to get your own way!'

It was hopeless. He would never understand.

'You haven't heard a word I've said, have you?'

'Then you'd better tell me again,' he said bitterly.

'But will you listen? Do you know how?'

She was implacable now — demanding his attention.

'I can't stand feeling a failure — and the way you make me feel worse . . . '

'Well, you have been pretty impossible.'

She supposed she had.

'I never thought things would turn out this way,' she said.

'It's been foreign ground for me too.'

So it had.

'I don't know that I've done all that well either,' he admitted, after a pause.

'What did we *want*, Paul?'

'Each other,' he replied, 'I suppose.'

'Well we got more than that, didn't we?'

'We did! Responsibility in spades. I wasn't prepared for that!'

There was a brief glimpse of something unexpected — of pressure, of worry.

'Do you mind?'

'What sort of question is that? How could I 'mind' about our children? Do *you*?'

'Of course not.'

'Well then . . . ' He looked at her sternly. 'We can surely do better than this. We have to.'

Oh, how Henry would approve of you, she

thought, with a quick flash of resentment. A man standing nobly by his commitments. No mention of love for me though. And if I ask him, how could I answer the reciprocal question?

So — there was nothing else to be done. I have no other option. Oh, Henry. Henry . . .

'If,' he was saying with some difficulty, 'if it would make things better — I will consider selling the house.'

'You mean it? You really mean it?'

'Of course I do.'

Perhaps then, there was no need to ask the question.

'Do you . . . ' she began, but he cut her short.

'Not now. We can talk about it later. I brought a salmon home for Andromeda to cook and she's panicking. I ought to go down.'

Salmon. His favourite dish.

'You'll need court bouillon and white wine,' Beth had told her. 'Only just enough to cover the fish. And only simmer it. Never let it boil.'

When he had brought salmon home for her to cook there had been no time to make the bouillon and inattention had often allowed the water to boil.

'Tell her not to worry,' she said, 'just look

after Barnaby. I will cook it.'

He looked at her, eyebrows raised and doubtful.

'Trust me,' she said.

He gave her a brief flick of a smile, touched her shoulder, and went downstairs.

When he had gone she faced herself in the mirror. Emotion does nothing for the appearance.

But the abiding beauty of bone and eye socket remained.

She set to work. She brushed back her heavy hair and twisted it to reveal the classical symmetry of skull. Somewhere there was a comb to hold it up. Lilac eye shadow. Just a touch. The Indian dress had been washed. Its soft folds were kind.

It did not take long.

She studied her reflection and smiled.

You'll do, she thought.

★　★　★

She cooked the salmon to perfection.

'Well, I never,' Andromeda said.

She also said, 'You've had quite a day. Why don't you go to bed early?'

'We'll both go,' Paul said.

24

The following morning she made breakfast for him. As he left the house they exchanged small, quick smiles.

Sleeping together again had been a wordless acceptance that this was what husbands and wives did and, since they were still husband and wife . . . No claims had been made and for this she was grateful; she was still too bruised and confused by recent encounters. Was he bruised? She wondered. He was certainly showing uncharacteristic confusion.

The morning was clean and clear. Sunlight poured in through the kitchen windows, setting copper saucepans aglow and striking diamond brilliance from the silver Andromeda was assiduously polishing.

'Leave that,' Catherine said impulsively. 'Let's blow bubbles for Barnaby.'

They stood him on the draining-board while Andromeda mixed the soapy water in the sink.

They watched, bewitched as the fragile, glistening shapes trembled out from between Andromeda's cupped thumb and forefinger and formed themselves into perfect, softly coloured transparent, floating balls of magic. The slight breeze lifted them and out through the window they went, dainty and steady, setting course for their journey.

'I've been thinking,' Andromeda ventured, her eyes still following their flight, and said no more.

'Well,' Catherine said impatiently. 'Are you waiting for congratulations? Do I pin a medal on you, Andromeda, the thinker?'

'I knew you'd go on.'

'I never 'go on'! Well — not at you, anyway.'

'That's just it,' the girl said uncomfortably. 'I don't listen on purpose — but I can't help hearing. I know how you feel about the children getting hurt in this house — and I know how Mr Grant . . . '

'Think no more,' Catherine silenced her quickly. 'We're selling it.' She was damned if she would discuss her private affairs. 'See to Barnaby.'

Andromeda obediently picked Barnaby up and strapped him into his bouncer. She retrieved a small woolly animal from where he had thrown it down and tied it round his ankle. 'There, give Wuff a go.' She set the ropes of the bouncer swinging and turned back to Catherine.

'No,' she said, as though in pain. 'No, you musn't do that! You're quite right about the children, but you musn't sell the house! That's what I've been thinking about.'

The girl was getting out of hand. The meek were at it again!

'And you're determined to tell me.'

'Yes. Then you can sack me if you like — I don't care — I just want . . . '

We don't get things we want, Catherine thought tightly, hasn't she learnt that yet? But Andromeda was looking so ernest and pleading it was impossible not to feel a twinge of compassion. And her intense blue gaze was as unrelenting as a searchlight.

'O-oh,' Catherine said, in exasperation. 'Stop looking at me like that. And I suppose you're going to go on and on . . . '

She did.

'You and me both,' Andromeda said. 'We're frightened they're going to fall over the gallery or down the staircase. Yes? Well, why do they have to go near there? Why can't they stay down here all the time?'

'Because the bedrooms are up there.'

'Ah,' She held up a finger. 'Think about it.'

'I can't see what there is . . . '

'You've never used that dining room since I've been here — and there's Mr Grant's study he hardly uses and that room where

268

you keep all your sewing and tapestry stuff. That's three rooms down here. They could be their bedrooms. You could block off the bottom of the . . . '

'How are we supposed to hear them if they cry in the night?'

'Well . . . ' she was looking less certain. 'There are three rooms — they don't need one each yet. There could be Jenny and Simon in one, me and Barnaby in another — and if you felt up to it, the third room could be made into their bathroom.'

'You mean you would move over into the house?'

The cheek of it! The unthinkable cheek.

'Then you could use my room as your office, if you wanted to get back into . . . '

She was unbelievable.

'Have you spoken to Mr Grant about this?'

'No! Of course not '

'Then don't! Just don't!'

'As if I'd . . . '

Barnaby was getting restless. He had run out of bounce and was fighting against the straps which held him.

Andromeda undid him and lifted him up. She turned and faced Catherine with him clasped in her arms.

'And that pool. It's not worth keeping it clean. You hardly go in — or Mr Grant. Why don't you drain it until the kids can swim? They ought to be learning now anyway; there's classes . . . '

'And what would that look like? A bloody great empty . . . '

'You could make a sunken garden of it for the time being. Big pots and statues and things. There was this article in *House and Garden*.'

'You *have* been thinking,' Catherine said acidly.

There was silence.

'I'll take him for his walk,' Andromeda said.

After they had gone Catherine stood in the silent kitchen and stared out of the window. Her mind was working rapidly. It took furniture up and down stairs, built an archway, chose which room could be the bathroom and wondered where she could find pots big enough. And don't let Andromeda dare suggest a statue of a simpering girl in a sunbonnet.

★ ★ ★

Nothing more on the subject was said when the girl and child returned.

★ ★ ★

Andromeda looked subdued and apprehen-
sive.

'Would you like to go up and see Mrs
Tims?' Catherine asked, 'I'll see about dinner
tonight, and Barnaby can go back to his own
bed.'

'Can you manage? Are you sure?'

Cold salmon, salad, peaches, cheese and
grapes, good coffee.

She was sure.

She had sudden thought.

'Your Mrs Tims. Is she a psychic?'

'A what?'

'You told me people come to see her for
help.'

'Oh, that. I don't know what — what you
said — is. She just — well, she just looks at
people and she seems to know.'

'Know what?'

'What they ought to do, I suppose.'

Catherine began to laugh.

'That makes two of you then.'

'I don't know what you mean.'

'Of course you don't.'

Catherine gave the stocky little shoulder an
affectionate biff. It was either that or take the
damn girl in her arms.

'You haven't thought, have you' Andromeda burst out, suddenly emboldened, 'what
the children would say when they're older

and find out you'd actually sold this house? They'd be mad. It will be perfect for them then — impress their friends, plenty of room to have them stay, parties round the pool . . . '

'Another word and I *will* sack you.' Catherine said.

But she was smiling.

★   ★   ★

'I'll take the trays out,' Paul said. 'Do you want coffee?'

'Please.'

He brought it in, black and strong, in two large mugs.

'This is more like it,' he said, and settled back beside her among the cushions.

They were more at peace together than they had been for a very long time.

'I have been thinking,' she said, cradling the mug.

She had thought so long and hard about Andromeda's ideas they had become her own and she saw nothing wrong in claiming them.

'How would it be if . . . '

She spelt it all out to him, careful detail after careful detail.

'We could use my money to put in the bathroom.'

272

'Oh, Cat.'

She had only seen him look so open and vulnerable on the morning Jenny was born.

'You don't know what that means to me.'

'You agree then?'

'Of course I do,' he laughed. 'I don't know about the pool though. It would be one hell of a sunken garden. But you're right. The children must learn to swim. You and Andromeda could take them for lessons in the week; we could take them together on the weekend.'

'You wouldn't mind Andromeda being . . . '

'She's around all the time anyway.'

'And that's all right with you?'

'Yes' He sounded surprised she should ask. 'She's a good kid.'

'You were against her being here at all.'

'Could you blame me? But she's proved herself and is looking more than halfway human now.'

Down to me, she thought.

'And she's willing — and efficient — and you can trust her. How often do you find someone like that?'

They took simultaneous sighs.

'Thank God that's over,' he said.

Stop thinking of it as being the end, make it the beginning. Henry had said.

'Another thing,' he said. 'It's just occured to me. I have to go to the States next week. Will you come with me? It could be just what we need.'

'But. . . '

'The children are with Beth and we know we can safely leave Barnaby with Andromeda.'

'But the house?'

'That too. Or we could invite Beth to come down with the children and stay with her.'

Doors were opening in the most unexpected fashion.

'No,' she said gently, after careful thought. 'Not this time. You'll be going again. Let's make it then. I'd like to be really fit . . . '

And to be able to wear my good clothes again — and to sparkle — fascinate his clients — be a credit to him. And to have laid my ghosts to rest. She smiled to herself. To think of that dear bulky figure as a ghost.

'If that's what you want.'

It was.

'Another thing,' It was just as well to have everything clear. 'I would like to go on seeing Janie.'

His face darkened. 'Don't push it.'

She did not have to think too long.

We will not be going to see Beth together, she decided, there will be no more golden days on the beach.

Janie would be hurt.

But somebody always has to be, she absolved herself, that's the way life is. I will have a word with Henry about her. And if that's not being selfless, what is?

'What are you thinking about?'

She turned her bland face to him.

'I was wondering when you will ring that man about the possum cages,' she said.

She settled back in her chair and took a long breath.

Things were going to be all right.

She did not expect she would find real happiness ahead, but at least it seemed she could relax within the safety of the marriage.

Grow up, Catherine, Henry had said. True safety is only found in oneself. Will I ever be grown up enough to find it?

Do other people? How many adults are there out there anyway?

Now she must provide safety for three small vulnerable people to whom it was a basic need.

And what will I be able to teach them?

Oh Henry, she thought.

Dear Henry.

As she knew she would think many times in the years to come, gratefully, but always with an enduring, wistful sense of loss.

We do hope that you have enjoyed reading this large print book.

Did you know that all of our titles are available for purchase?

We publish a wide range of high quality large print books including:
Romances, Mysteries, Classics
General Fiction
Non Fiction and Westerns

Special interest titles available in large print are:
The Little Oxford Dictionary
Music Book
Song Book
Hymn Book
Service Book

Also available from us courtesy of Oxford University Press:
Young Readers' Dictionary
(large print edition)
Young Readers' Thesaurus
(large print edition)

For further information or a free brochure, please contact us at:
Ulverscroft Large Print Books Ltd.,
The Green, Bradgate Road, Anstey,
Leicester, LE7 7FU, England.
Tel: (00 44) **0116 236 4325**
Fax: (00 44) **0116 234 0205**

Other titles in the
Ulverscroft Large Print Series:

STRANGER IN THE PLACE

Anne Doughty

Elizabeth Stewart, a Belfast student and only daughter of hardline Protestant parents, sets out on a study visit to the remote west coast of Ireland. Delighted as she is by the beauty of her new surroundings and the small community which welcomes her, she soon discovers she has more to learn than the details of the old country way of life. She comes to reappraise so much that is slighted and dismissed by her family — not least in regard to herself. But it is her relationship with a much older, Catholic man, Patrick Delargy, which compels her to decide what kind of life she really wants.

EVERY GOOD GIRL

Judy Astley

After twenty years of marriage, Nina had offloaded serial philanderer Joe and was happy coping alone with their two demanding daughters. But some disturbing elements began to appear in her new, carefree life. A flasher had been accosting young girls on the nearby common. Home no longer felt so safe. And Joe, during one of his oh-so-civilised monthly lunches with Nina, revealed that the new love in his life, power-dressed Catherine, had decided that she now required a baby. But babies, Joe told Nina, were what he did with her: a remark that Nina found oddly unsettling . . .

A FANCY TO KILL FOR

Hilary Bonner

Richard Corrington is rich, handsome and a household name. But is he sane . . . ? When journalist Joyce Carter is murdered only a few miles from Richard's west country home, his wife suspects he has been having an affair with her, and forensics implicate him in the killing. But Detective Chief Inspector Todd Mallett believes that Joyce's murder is part of something much more sinister and complex. There have been other deaths; the senseless killing of a young woman on a Cornish beach, another in a grim London subway . . . And somewhere on the Exmoor hills a killer waits. Stalking his prey. Ready to strike again . . .

RUN WILD MY HEART

Maureen Child

For beautiful Margaret Allen, travelling alone across the western plains was her only escape from a loveless marriage — a marriage secretly arranged by her father as part of a heartless business scheme. In a fury, she left her quiet, unassuming life behind and ventured out on her own . . . Cheyenne Boder set out to claim a cash reward for finding Margaret and bringing her home. But the handsome frontiersman found a promise of love in her sweet smile and vowed to unearth the hidden passions that made her a bold, proud woman of the west!